7/06

THE BILLIONAIRE'S BRIDE

BY

JACKIE BRAUN

MILLS & BOON®

For my sisters Donna, Patty and Loraine

First published in Great Britain 2005
Large Print edition 2006
Harlequin Mills & Boon Limited,
Eton House, 18-24 Paradise Road,
Richmond, Surrey TW9 1SR

© Jackie Braun Fridline 2005

ISBN 0 263 18928 7

Set in Times Roman 17½ on 20 pt.
16-0106-42290

Printed and bound in Great Britain
by Antony Rowe Ltd, Chippenham, Wiltshire

PROLOGUE

MARNIE STRIKER LARUE covered the mouthpiece of the telephone with one hand and hollered, "Do *not* put Dorothy in the fridge again, Noah."

She couldn't see into the kitchen, but she'd developed a sixth sense where her four-year-old son was concerned and he'd been awfully preoccupied with that goldfish lately.

Sure enough, he hollered back, "Aw, Mom."

When Marnie saw him dash in the direction of his bedroom, she settled back onto the couch beside the mountain of unfolded laundry and, securing the receiver between her ear and shoulder, said, "So, what were you about to say, Mother?"

"I just wanted to mention that Dad saw an interesting article in the *Phoenix Sun* the other day about how the number of female-owned businesses is on the rise."

Apparently her parents, who had retired to Arizona several years before, still had a sixth sense when it came to their youngest child.

This was another not so subtle reminder that Marnie's plan to start her own business had languished for three years now. With her late husband's enthusiastic backing, she'd plotted out a strategy for a mail-order business, a frillier version of Land's End and L.L. Bean. At first, she'd planned to offer clothing and accessories for women like her who lived far from shopping centers and strip malls, but who still wanted to be fashionable. Later, she'd hoped to branch out into men's and children's clothing and then finally to include home decor.

It was to be called Marnie's Closet, a name that had come courtesy of her sister-in-law,

Rose, who still borrowed things to wear on occasion, although not as often now since Marnie hadn't added so much as a new belt to her wardrobe in a few seasons.

The entire typed-out plan was still somewhere in Marnie's house, gathering dust. It had been hatched PHD—Pre-Hal's Death. That's how Marnie thought of everything now, as if her world had been bisected neatly in two by the events of one horrific afternoon three years earlier.

"Your husband is dead."

Those were the only words she'd heard that day. The remainder of what the kind-faced Michigan State Police officer had said had been lost to the roaring in her ears as she'd sat on the couch in her tidy little home holding tightly to her infant son while the rest of her world had slipped beyond her grasp and shattered into unsalvageable pieces.

Even now it seemed inconceivable. Dead? Not Hal. Not her careful, methodical, safety-conscious husband. It was a mistake. Had to be. Someone else's husband had died trying to save two inebriated downstate snowmobilers who had ignored thin ice warnings and tumbled sled and all into the unforgiving waters of Lake Superior.

But then as now the truth could not be ignored. Hal was dead. The boy she had loved, the young man she had married, had become the spouse she mourned.

Since his death, she'd forgotten all about the business venture that had so excited her. She'd forgotten about everything but maintaining her tenuous financial footing and seeing to her son's needs. Every morning for the past three years she'd gotten up tired and every night she had gone to bed bone weary, the monotony of her predictable schedule broken only by the bittersweet joy of watching her son learn to walk and talk and then run and reason.

"You know, they have a lot of programs to

help women entrepreneurs succeed," her mother said.

Marnie closed her eyes and counted to ten before replying blandly, "Really. That's interesting."

She was determined not to rise to the bait. But her mother was a master angler and not about to let her daughter off the hook so easily.

"It's a shame you haven't given it any more thought. You do a wonderful job running the Lighthouse Tavern for Mason while he's out of town."

Marnie's older brother was a state legislator now. She had taken over his managerial duties at their family-owned pub when he was elected to the state House a few years back. What her mother wasn't saying in this carefully choreographed conversation was what they all knew: Marnie found running the tavern safe and familiar.

The woman who previously had craved adventure and excitement had not strayed from the beaten path since she'd opened the door that chilly March afternoon to two grim-looking state troopers and become a single mother grappling to make ends meet.

"Why don't you bring Noah down to see us over Easter break?" her mother suggested. "The change of scenery would do you both good."

"It's not a good time, Mom."

Marnie switched the telephone receiver to her other shoulder and continued to fold laundry. It seemed like one endless, thankless chore to her. From the corner of her eye, she watched the source of much of that laundry streak by, peanut butter and jelly smeared on his shirt as well as his face. Noah was on his second outfit of the day and it wasn't quite one o'clock.

"Nonsense. It's the perfect time for you to come. Mason will be back in town over the holidays. The Legislature is out of session."

"I'm sorry, Mom. But I really can't afford a vacation right now."

But her mother persisted. "Dad and I want to see our grandson. And you, too, dear. Come out to Arizona. It's our treat."

"I can't let you pay our airfare."

Indignation turned her voice crisp. She earned a living, enough to pay her bills on time if she was frugal. She had yet to touch a penny of Hal's life insurance policy, which she'd invested for Noah, to be used to finance his college education. And she would be damned if she'd accept a handout now simply because her mother thought she needed to put her feet up.

But her indignation was short lived.

"We're your parents, Marnie Elizabeth, so don't you dare think of it as charity," her mother said sternly.

The tone she used had Marnie cringing. She was thousands of miles away and yet her mother could always make Marnie feel just as she had when she was a twelve and had been caught smoking dried corn silk out behind the woodshed. She'd been grounded for two weeks—the fact that she'd turned green and thrown up apparently not punishment enough in Edith Striker's estimation.

"We either pay your airfare to come here or we pay our airfare to come there. Same amount either way, so which will it be?"

Before she could respond, her mother threw down the trump card.

"Of course, with Dad's arthritis, Michigan's cold weather will be hell on his joints, but I'll leave the choice up to you."

Some choice.

But after hanging up, Marnie resigned herself to the visit, deciding there were worse things than having to spend time in a warm climate during the last leg of northern Michigan's harsh winter. Besides, it would be good for Noah. He deserved a little fun and adventure now and then.

She began mentally making plans for a two-week stay at her parents' home just outside Yuma. She'd have to get someone to pick up her mail, water the houseplants and feed Noah's goldfish—assuming the poor thing survived until then. Glancing at the piles of folded laundry, she realized she'd also have to sort through her son's summer clothes to see what still fit.

Maybe she could pick up a few things for him down in Arizona. Maybe she could pick up a few things for herself. Getting more in the spirit of things, she decided the trip might be good for her, an unexpected detour of sorts before she returned to her life's monotony.

CHAPTER ONE

"HOLA! UM...UH...HMM.

"*Donde esta...? Donde esta...?* What's the word?" she muttered. Glancing up at the clearly baffled cafe owner, she asked hopefully, "Bathroom? Um. *Toileto? El johno?*"

Okay, so it wasn't actual Spanish, but Marnie really had to use the facilities and it couldn't wait until after she'd rewound the Berlitz tape she'd listened to in the car on the trip south from Arizona and figured out the word for rest room.

Some detour, Marnie thought, as she thumbed through her Spanish/English dictionary in desperation. She hadn't planned this side trip to Mexico, but she'd felt so crowded at her parents' Yuma, Arizona, home. She was a grown woman of thirty-two, a mother herself to a precocious preschooler. But for four days they had hovered over her as if she were a wounded chick in need of nurturing. Finally she 'd decided to leave Noah in their care—he would appreciate the doting, after all. She'd borrowed their car and driven south with no destination in mind.

Now, here she was a couple of hours or so beyond the United States border on Mexico's Baja Peninsula. And she really needed to relieve herself.

From behind her, she heard the deep rumble of masculine laughter. When she turned, Marnie wondered how she could have missed the man. He sat at one of the small round tables near the door, his hulking frame in silhouette thanks to the light streaming in from the window behind him. And yet she knew without clearly seeing his features that his expression was one of amusement.

At her expense.

"Do you speak English?" she demanded, squelching the urge to cross her legs and hop in place.

"*Si, yo hablo ingles, muchacha,*" he replied smoothly.

His pronunciation was so flawless it took her a moment to realize that while he'd said so in Spanish, he could indeed communicate with her.

She pasted on a smile—one that would have had her brother Mason wisely moving well out of her range. This man merely crossed his arms over his broad chest and leaned back until the front legs of his chair left the ground.

"Clever, Mr.—?"

Where her lethal glare hadn't fazed him, her simple question apparently did. The chair bounced back to the ground with a thud. He hesitated a moment, as if he was reluctant to identify himself.

"Friends call me J.T," he said at last.

"J.T. Wow, that's funny."

He angled his head to one side, again seeming suspicious of her. "What's funny?"

"Just that we're barely acquaintances and I already have a pet name for you, too."

But she bit her tongue on the expletive that came to mind and asked sweetly, "So, J.T., could you tell me where the rest room is?" Her smile was really more a baring of teeth when she added, *"Por favor."*

"Donde esta el baño?"

"Yes, yes." She waved her hand impatiently. "I think we've already established that you're bilingual. And isn't that a wonderful trait? I know I now deeply regret taking Home Ec as an elective rather than a foreign language while I was in high school. Be that as it may, I'd really appreciate it right now if you could just answer the question. In English. Or maybe French. I did take two semesters of French in middle school."

He rattled off something that had her exhaling slowly. The man *would* have to be multilingual.

"Okay, not French. English. English!"

"Well, then, by all means."

He stood and took a few steps toward her, bringing him close enough that she could now fully make out his features. Where she and Hal had been on eye level, this man had several inches on her, despite the thick wedge of her heel. He was blond to her dark hair, with eyes the same shade of blue as the flower of the wild chicory that grew alongside the highway back home. Every inch of him was tanned and toned, and impressively coated with some serious muscle.

Not her type at all, she thought, even as her pulse rate spiked and almost made her forget the fact that her bladder felt as if it were being stretched by the entire contents of the Great Lakes.

It had been a long time since she'd felt this way around a member of the opposite sex.

The sensation was unwanted now, and, to Marnie's way of thinking, its presence was just another reason to dislike the handsome stranger.

"Down that hallway and to the right."

"Thank you."

"*De nada.*"

She smiled and had just taken a step in the direction he'd indicated when he added, "For future reference, *Donde esta el baño?* is handy phrase should you find yourself in your, uh, current predicament again."

"*Gracias,*" she replied with a roll of her eyes and hurriedly took her leave.

The annoying, albeit gorgeous American was nowhere to be found when Marnie returned, a fact for which she was grateful. The exchange made her feel foolish now. And she didn't care for that instant jolt of attraction. She didn't like his type, good-looking though he was. She preferred men with brains to men with mere brawn.

The woman wiping up the tables in the cafe smiled broadly when Marnie approached. After a long consultation with the dictionary, she was able to ask about accommodations. The woman pointed to the map Marnie held, her slim finger stopping just north of the small fishermen's village where they were. Marnie had passed through the resort town the woman indicated. She'd wanted no part of it. Too loud. Too crowded. She wanted peace and quiet and a bit of isolation. This small village place was perfect.

"No, no. No…*turista*."

She flipped through the book again. She'd bought it less than twenty-four hours earlier and it was already dog-eared and showing other signs of wear. Well, she was definitely getting her money's worth.

"I need to get away, be alone," Marnie said in English, knowing full well the woman's polite smile meant she didn't have a clue what she was rattling on about.

"Viuda," Marnie said finally, pressing a hand to her heart as she uttered the Spanish word for widow.

"Ah," the woman replied, brown eyes melting with sympathy. It was the last thing Marnie wanted right now. She had enough of that in Chance Harbor. After Hal's death, it was as if her name had changed from Marnie LaRue to Marnie Poor Thing.

"I need…" She flipped through pages. *"Tranquilidad."*

"Si, si," the woman bobbed her head.

Half an hour later, Marnie was back in her car and trying to follow the crude map the woman's husband had drawn for her. His English had been only slightly better than Marnie's Spanish, which obviously wasn't saying much. But he'd assured her that the small house of his *abuela,* which Marnie thought meant grandmother, was quiet and secluded and overlooked the Pacific.

It sounded perfect. The homeowner had

moved in with family. She was too old to live alone any longer, the man had told Marnie. As the road opened up and her beachfront accommodations for the extended weekend came into view, Marnie thought she understood why.

She no longer felt guilty about the ridiculously low sum she'd paid to rent the place. It was little more than a shack built just back from the large boulders that dotted the beach, with rooms haphazardly tacked on at various angles to the original structure. A hundred yards down the beach, she spied another home. This one was a little more reputable-looking, but any hope she'd held out that it might be the place was dashed when she spied the black Jeep Wrangler parked outside.

It was only four days, she reminded herself. Then she took in the incredible view and decided the panoramic of the Pacific more than made up for any shortcomings in her accommodations. What did it matter where she slept or took her meals as long as she got to wake up to that?

Marnie had always loved the water. Even after Hal's drowning death in Lake Superior, she'd continued to find being near it peaceful, restorative—essential even. Something about its vast size and rhythm soothed her, even on days when the lake's surface was puckered with waves.

The ocean, so much bigger than even the greatest of the Great Lakes, had that soothing rhythm as well. She parked the car and walked to where the water churned white at shore. Seabirds swooped and called overhead, and even though it was only about seventy degrees, the air was heavy and seemed warmer thanks to a salty humidity that had her licking her lips to see if she could taste it. She could.

A storm was coming. Farther out, dark clouds were gathering, roiling in hues of purple and gray on the horizon. She should unpack her belongings. At the very least, she should unload the groceries she'd purchased at the market in town. But she tucked the keys in the front pocket of her shorts, tugged off her sandals and walked to where her feet flirted with the surf.

Now, here she was.

La Playa de la Pisada. Footprint Beach. That was the name of the small village she'd stumbled across. As Marnie added her own footprints to the sand, she knew coming here had been a good idea.

An hour later, as the first fat drops of rain turned into a torrent, she revised her opinion. The roof leaked, big time. The electricity was iffy, shutting off with a threatening sizzle with every gust of wind. So far it kept sputtering back on a few moments later, but she wasn't sure how long her luck would hold. All of this was small potatoes compared to the roommate she'd discovered living in the primitive bathroom. Marnie had shrieked with unholy abandon when she'd spied the small scaly critter and then slammed the door closed. It could stay there. She didn't need a bathroom.

¿Donde esta el baño?

The phrase came back to her, as did the memory of the man who'd uttered it. What was his story? she wondered, telling herself it was simple curiosity that had her recalling his Brad Pitt jaw line and impossibly blue eyes. He wasn't a local, at least not originally. American like her and maybe, like her, he'd come seeking peace and quiet.

The electricity sizzled off again, but at least the rain was letting up some. Marnie decided she could do without the quiet part just now. She hopped over mud puddles on the way to her car and cranked up the volume on the stereo. The humble bungalow didn't have a radio let alone a compact disk player.

As Marvin Gaye sang of sexual healing, Marnie went back inside to unpack her belongings. The knock on the open door a few minutes later startled her as she stacked a few canned goods in the cupboard. When she turned, the man from the café stood just outside in the drizzle. While his lips had twitched with laughter at their last meeting, this time they were drawn into a tight line.

"Just who in the hell are you?" he asked abruptly, stepping over the threshold.

The electricity came back on then, the overhead light in the kitchen flickering to life as if sparked by his mere presence.

At five-ten, Marnie wasn't what anyone would classify as petite. She was in good enough shape to have tone to her muscles, but she was no body builder. What she was at this moment, she realized as fear pooled in the pit of her stomach, was a lone female in a foreign country with no telephone service and far enough from civilization that no one would hear her scream. So, she picked up the first object she could find—one of her sandals—and, summoning up some bravado, brandished it in the man's handsome face.

"I suggest you stay away from me."

He blinked in surprise, raising a hand to shove damp sandy hair back from his eyes.

"You're threatening me with a shoe?"

"It's got a heel and I'm not afraid to use it," she bluffed in a deadly serious tone even though she knew there was nothing lethal about the sandal's cork wedge.

"Who are you?" he asked again, this time seeming more baffled than angry.

"A woman who doesn't want to be messed with, *amigo*." Fear took a distant second to irritation as she stepped forward, poked a finger into the brick wall of his chest and challenged, "Who are you?"

"I think you know."

"J.T.," Marnie replied, repeating the initials the man gave her during their last encounter.

"Yes, J.T.," he drawled. "Now, who sent you?"

"Sent me?"

"Whom do you work for?"

"I work for myself," Marnie replied.

It was true, sort of. She was a waitress and sometimes manager at her family's tavern, and, as her family could attest, no one told her what to do.

But I could be doing more, a little voice hummed. She lifted her chin and ignored it.

"So, you're a freelancer."

Blinking slowly, she regarded the man. She had no clue what he was blathering on about, but she lowered the shoe. If he'd planned to assault her, surely he would have done so by now without playing twenty questions first.

"What in heaven's name are you talking about?" she asked in exasperation.

Before he could answer, the critter in the bathroom thumped against the door.

"What the devil?"

J.T. stepped around Marnie in the small kitchen and headed toward the equally miniscule adjoining room that probably served as the home's main gathering place, although at the moment it had no furnishings. He pointed to the closed door at the far end of the room.

"What do you have in there?"

"No idea. I opened the bathroom door and there it was. I wasn't going to evict it."

Marnie smiled at J.T., ready to forgive him for his rudeness now that she had determined he was quite harmless: annoying, arrogant and appallingly short on manners, but harmless nonetheless.

She was still smiling when she asked, "Maybe you could, um, convince it to go outside?"

Then she handed him the shoe.

J.T. couldn't believe this woman. She had the sultry, sexy look of a lingerie model: long, slender limbs, a well-curved bottom and generous bust, all neatly topped off with a short dark mop of hair, deep brown eyes and lips that looked inviting even when she was snarling at him. She was a study in contrasts, much like the Baja peninsula with its deserts, mountains and gorgeous coastline. One minute she was threatening him with a flimsy sandal and the next she was trying to wheedle a favor out of him.

And she still hadn't answered his question.

"Tell me who you are and why you're here, and I'll consider doing my best imitation of the Crocodile Hunter for you," he bartered.

She heaved an aggravated sigh that had the thin material of her cotton T-shirt pulling taut across her chest, drawing J.T.'s attention. He tried his best not to think about how long it had been since he'd spent some quality time alone with a woman.

"Fine. I'm Marnie. Marnie LaRue of Chance Harbor, Michigan."

"The plates on your vehicle say Arizona."

"My folks live there. I borrowed their car. Satisfied?"

"Hardly. Why are *you* here?"

Marnie. Was that a real name? he wondered. A pen name? It had a certain exotic quality about it, much like the woman herself.

"Why are you here?" she countered.

He crossed his arms over his chest. "Uh-uh-uh. I'll ask the questions."

"Control freak," he thought he heard her mutter before she admitted, "I'm in Mexico for a little R and R."

"Please. You can lie better than that. Rest and recreation are what they specialize in up the highway from here. Despite its picturesque name and stunning view, La Playa de la Pisada isn't a mecca for tourists," he said. And, as if to underscore his point, the creature in the bathroom thumped against the door again.

He pointed toward the door and offered a mocking smile. "Exhibit A."

"I never said I was a tourist."

He nodded in satisfaction. "Finally we're getting somewhere."

"I'm not here for a vacation. I'm here for some…solitude."

J.T. exhaled sharply in frustration. "A woman who looks like you doesn't come to a place like this for solitude or anything else."

"Where would a woman who looks like me go?" she asked and he got the impression she was trying to figure out if he meant the description as a compliment or an insult.

He pointed to her luggage. It was as bright red as newly spilled blood and about the size of a small car.

"I'll bet there's not one pair of sensible shoes or jeans in there. Hell, I'll bet there's nothing practical in there, period."

"Care to put money on that wager?"

"Why not?" J.T. shot back, amused.

He pulled out his wallet and then immediately regretted his impulsiveness when her eyes widened at the thick wad of American bills he carried. He tugged out a twenty and tucked the wallet away.

Motioning with his chin, he said, "Open it."

She unzipped the overstuffed bag with an aggressive yank of her arm and tossed back the lid. As she rummaged around inside its contents, colorful swatches of silk and satin caught J.T.'s attention. Lingerie model, he thought again. She damn well could be with all the mouthwatering unmentionables she had stowed in her bag. But he reminded himself that the frothy contents only confirmed his suspicions. No one who looked like Marnie came to this tiny little backwater in Mexico with a suitcase full of soft, frilly, feminine things to rent a shack of a house and seek *solitude.*

She had another motive, and he'd bet his last buck it wasn't so pure. He'd had his fill of inquisitive women, whether they were reporters seeking an exclusive interview or job applicants eager to skip his company's personnel department and dazzle him directly with their resumes.

Worst of all, though, were the marriage-minded mercenaries who had hunted him relentlessly since his divorce became final two years earlier. None of them had ever managed to find him here, though. He'd been careful, very careful, to cover his tracks.

Still, J.T. wasn't sure which category Marnie fit into. She didn't seem to be trying to impress him with her charm, wit and appealing ass…um…assets.

Maybe she wasn't a gold digger. A reporter? He'd never met one who hadn't skewered him with a dozen questions before offering a business card. As for a job applicant, she didn't seem the sort to dabble in software design. Okay, maybe he was stereotyping here, but not many of the women who worked at Tracker Operating Systems looked like something that stepped out of one of those glossy fashion magazines that sported more advertisements than editorial content.

As he mulled the possibilities, Marnie extracted something from her bag with an exaggerated flourish.

"Tell me this isn't practical," she challenged, holding up the item with one hand as she settled the other one on her hip.

J.T. tried to keep a straight face. Really, he tried. He was known for his cool demeanor and unreadable expression, after all. But how could he be expected to maintain a serious facade when faced with this? Sure, the flashlight she'd produced had practical written all over it. Problem was it also had a skimpy little swatch of black lace snagged on its switch.

"Which is intended as the turn-on?" he couldn't resist asking.

The room was relatively gloomy, illuminated by only one small lamp and the last remnants of evening light that streamed in from the small window that faced the ocean. And yet when she glanced at the flashlight and caught sight of the flirty little thong dangling from it, he swore she blushed scarlet.

His amusement was cut short however. Barely a heartbeat later, lightning flashed outside, followed swiftly by a deafening clap of thunder. The room's lone lamp sizzled briefly before sputtering out, leaving them in virtual darkness.

Marnie flipped on the flashlight, all but blinding J.T. with its penetrating beam.

"Practical," she said succinctly. And held out one hand. "Now pay up."

A couple of hours later, J.T. stretched out on the plush mattress of his king-size bed, but he couldn't get comfortable. His thoughts had strayed to Marnie LaRue and stayed there.

He'd roused the harmless lizard from the shack's bathroom and then had left her in darkness. He still felt guilty about it and as if his mother would pop out of the woodwork at any moment and berate him for his lack of chivalry. But until he knew who Marnie was and what she was after, he planned to keep her at arm's length.

From the outside, his home looked barely more habitable than the one Marnie was renting. J.T. intended it that way. No one would guess a billionaire vacationed there when he really needed to get away. And he really needed to get away right now, what with the government threatening an antitrust lawsuit.

He heaved a sigh and reached for the remote on the nightstand. With a click of a button, Smokey Robinson was singing about the tears of a clown. Despite the home's rough exterior, the inside was another story. The furnishings of its six rooms were state-of-the-art, from the stainless steel six-burner oven and wine cooler in the kitchen, to the plush leather upholstery in the living room and the elaborate computer setup in the den.

When he'd returned that evening, he'd booted up his computer—thanks to a backup generator, he never lost power. And thanks to the onward march of technology, even in this small outpost, he had access to the Internet. A Google search had turned up nothing on Ms. LaRue. Chance Harbor, Michigan, had scored a few hits, but nothing that really told J.T. anything useful except that she had at least given him the name of a real city, tiny though it was.

And that only turned up more questions. She said she'd come here for quiet and isolation. Couldn't she get that without leaving home? Chance Harbor was located about as far north as one could go in Michigan without taking a dip in Lake Superior. And the population of that bustling metropolis: 793.

Something didn't add up. J.T. wasn't deterred. His company's logo was a bloodhound—specifically, Tracker, the beloved dog he'd had as a boy. J.T. would figure it out. He was determined to rework the numbers until they did add up.

* * *

Marnie spied the lights at the house just up the beach, the place where she assumed J.T. now sat enjoying his evening. Was he renting it, too? If so, he'd gotten the better deal. It didn't appear to be much larger than the one she was paying for, and it hardly looked more habitable, but it had electricity at this point, whereas she had nothing but a fire in the primitive hearth to roast hot dogs over.

God, she hated hot dogs. But she'd brought them with her in the small cooler she'd packed because they were easy. The perfect multipurpose food. No one knew better than the mother of a finicky four-year-old how quickly boiling water, a bon fire or a gas grill could turn pressed meat into a meal. And Noah loved them.

Truth be told, she wasn't much of a cook. Never had been. In fact, Hal had prepared most of the meals during their marriage, for which she was eternally grateful. Still, surviving on her own cooking did have one nice side benefit. At least she never had to watch her weight.

She pulled the blackened dog from the fire and sighed. Nope. No calories to worry about here.

Marnie tossed her dinner into the fire, stood up and stretched. She really wasn't that hungry anyway. Without bothering to locate the flashlight, she stumbled to the home's only bedroom and felt her way along in the dark until her knee rapped smartly against the bed's wooden footboard.

With a sigh of exhaustion, she flopped onto the lumpy, unmade mattress still wearing her clothes, too tired to bother to hunt up her toothbrush or take out her gritty-feeling contact lenses.

Sleep. When she didn't have any of the disruptions or responsibilities of motherhood to intrude, Marnie Striker LaRue was remarkably good at it.

CHAPTER TWO

BRIGHT beams of light stretched through the unadorned window the following morning, rousing Marnie from sleep. She ignored them, or tried to, rolling over and reaching for the covers only to discover the small bed had none.

"So much for sleeping in," she muttered.

Her eyelids fluttered opened, dried up contacts making her blink rapidly to clear the film over her vision, and then she glanced around the small, sparsely furnished room, perplexed. She had just two thoughts.

Where was she?

And, was there any coffee?

She stumbled to the window and smiled as

her memory returned. Just yards away, the ocean rose up in gentle swells before spilling itself on the beach.

La Playa de la Pisada.

She supposed she should find a pay phone. Her cell didn't work here. She needed to call her folks, check on her son. She knew he was in good care. Actually, she thought with a smile, it was her parents she worried about. Noah could be quite a handful when he wanted to get his own way, which tended to be all of the time.

Her stomach growled loudly, reminding her of the need for food and the fact that she had not eaten dinner the night before. But more than anything, she wanted a hot shower and that first glorious jolt of caffeine.

It was just her rotten luck, Marnie decided, that the electricity was still off and the water coming out of the faucet in the bathroom was a rusty brown color and cold to boot.

Well, no sense complaining about it, especially since she was alone and doing so wouldn't accomplish anything. She settled for a glass of lukewarm juice and a slice of buttered bread. Then she pulled on the swimsuit she'd brought to Arizona for her parents' pool and slathered on sunscreen.

As she passed the car parked just outside, she flipped on its stereo, sliding in a CD of Aretha Franklin's greatest hits before heading down to the beach. A quick dip would clear the cobwebs, especially since the water was bound to be cool. But she'd grown up on Lake Superior, which was hypothermia-inducing even in August. She was no stranger to cold water, but that really wasn't the main attraction anyway. Give her a beach, a towel and a block of free time, and she could sunbathe with the best of them. She figured she'd earned a couple hours of lazing around before she went into town. It had been ages since she'd last stretched out on sand with nothing more pressing to do than flip over every so often to keep her tan even.

Besides, hadn't her own mother said she needed a vacation? Marnie planned to make the most of her break from responsibility.

The morning air was cool on her exposed skin, but the sun's warmth was already promising. She was just spreading her towel out when J.T. startled her by saying, "If you're planning to go in, I hope you're a good swimmer. There can be a nasty undertow around here, and I'm not going to jump in and save you."

As if she would accept his help anyway, she thought sourly, but when she turned to tell him so, the words died on her lips. Forget the sexy, wind-tossed blond hair, stubble of sandy beard and well-muscled arms. What really had her mouth watering was what he held in his hand.

"Is that coffee?"

He drank deeply before replying, apparently having noted the reverence in her tone.

"Yes it is."

"Black? No sugar or flavored creamer or anything?"

"Why mess with a good thing?" he replied, and she agreed completely.

"You wouldn't happen to have more of it?"

"An entire pot. Just made it before I came out for my morning walk." He sipped it again and she swore her mouth began to water. "Ground the beans myself. Starbucks, French roast."

She couldn't help it. A soft moan escaped her lips. He raised his eyebrows when he heard it, but he made no comment.

"I don't suppose you're feeling...neighborly?"

He smiled, and Marnie told herself it was only the promise of caffeine that had her pulse shooting off like a bottle rocket. Certainly, it wasn't the more than six feet of gorgeous man standing five yards in front of her, wearing tan cargo shorts and a wrinkled white T-shirt that appeared to be on inside out, as if it had been pulled on hastily.

"Is that a yes?" She tipped her head to one side and offered a slow, sensual smile in return. Two could play his game, she decided.

His gaze lingered on her lips before dipping lower, lower. She almost felt caressed by his thorough, frank appraisal. And she figured she had him.

Marnie didn't believe in false modesty, so she would be the first to say she looked damned good in this swimsuit, great even. It hid the small tummy she'd gained since Noah, the little pouch that no amount of sit-ups seemed to eradicate. She'd come to grips with that and had decided to work around it. Accentuate the positive, as the saying went. And so she did. The neckline scooped low to show off her full breasts, and the bottom was cut high at the hip to reveal every inch of her long and slender—if a bit pale at this point—legs.

She'd planned to carry this suit and dozens

of other flattering ones in her mail-order business in what she now thought of as her other life. And even though she'd purchased it three years ago, this was the first time she'd actually worn it outside the confines of a fitting room or in her bedroom, where she'd taken pleasure in modeling it for her husband just a month before the accident.

J.T.'s voice snapped her back to the present.

"Sorry, I'm not in a generous mood today."

He didn't bother to hide his smile after he took another satisfying gulp.

She scowled at him. All that flirting wasted.

"Just today? I got the feeling that was a permanent state for you," she snapped.

"Why are you here?"

"Again with the questions," she groused, sliding her feet out of her sandals and dumping her sunglasses onto the towel.

"I haven't liked any of the answers so far," he shot back.

"Your problem."

The breeze tugged at her hair when she turned away from him and started toward the water.

"I meant it about the undertow," he called after her.

She was hip deep in the chilly water before she replied, "Yes, but did you mean the part about not coming in to save me?"

J.T. watched her dive under the next wave. Her dark head emerged a few feet away and then went under again. He scanned the surf between large rock formations, anxious for a glimpse of her, but spotted nothing.

"Damn!" he muttered, setting his coffee down on one of the rocks and tugging the shirt he wore over his head.

He was in the water, swimming frantically toward the spot where he'd last spied her, when he heard laughter. Treading water, he turned and saw her standing on the beach.

Holding his coffee cup.

She raised it in mock salute before bringing

it to her smiling lips. Afterward, she called, "You make a mean cup of joe, J.T."

She was still laughing as he swam to shore. By the time he reached her towel, where she sat reclining on her elbows, wet skin glistening in the morning sun, his coffee cup had been drained and J.T. had worked his way past irritated to the upper end of irate.

"That stunt was incredibly low, not to mention stupid. If there had been an undertow, I could have drowned trying to save your sorry butt."

"I beg to differ."

"About the undertow?"

"No, about my butt. It is anything but sorry," she said.

He opened his mouth, then snapped it back shut. He wanted to argue with her. Really, he wanted to. But she had a point. In fact, he'd spent several hours the night before lying in his bed thinking about the very butt in question as well as the rest of the package that, when put together, made up one mouthwatering woman.

Still, he wasn't letting her off the hook, no matter how fine he found that derriere.

"I'd like an apology."

She tipped down her sunglasses and regarded him over the top of the dark lenses. Even without a hint of makeup, she had the most incredible eyes. They made him think of molasses. They were that dark and rich, and when she blinked she did so slowly, as if it were an effort to close the lids.

"I'll admit to being ruthless when it comes to my morning coffee, but you will recall that I asked you very nicely to share before resorting to trickery."

"Trickery? Try thievery."

She shrugged as if to concede the point. "Call the cops."

"That's it? That's all you have to say?" he demanded.

"No. That's not all." She glanced at the hem

of his soaking wet shorts. "You're dripping on my towel."

She had the audacity to slide the sunglasses up the bridge of her nose and lay back on the towel.

J.T.'s control was the stuff of legends. He never lost his cool, not during the most heated of board meetings, not even during his divorce settlement, when Terri's team of lawyers had hovered like vultures over his self-made fortune and tried to pick off what they could.

But looking down at the smug raven-haired woman, he lost something. He didn't think. He didn't consider the consequences—something his attorney would ream him for were Richard Danton present. No, J.T. acted. Bending down, he scooped Marnie up from her towel and headed toward the ocean, intent on dumping her into the churning surf.

That'll teach her to mess with me, he thought.

"What do you think you're doing?" she cried.

Oh, he had her plenty surprised. She squirmed in arms, cool wet flesh sliding against cool wet flesh until the friction generated heat.

Lots and lots of heat.

And now she wasn't the only one surprised. Beneath his anger, he felt it, that low tug of something he didn't want to feel at all. But there it was, and there was no denying its existence.

Marnie wasn't a small woman. Tall, long-limbed, nicely curved in all of the areas that counted. She filled up his arms almost as well as she filled out her bathing suit.

And, she had one hell of a right hook he realized too late.

It connected solidly with his jaw, staggered him so that they both wound up sprawled in the sand. A wave came up, cool water drenching the pair of them, but this was hardly like the scene in *From Here to Eternity*. Neither of the actors in that movie had taken one on the chin before going down.

"What was that for?"

"As if you need to ask," she spat, disengaging her legs from his and then rolling to her feet.

She glared down at him, an angry Amazon. God, he'd never seen any woman look half as sexy. And that thought made him more determined to ignore his traitorous libido.

He didn't have time for this distraction in his life right now. He had enough on his plate with the Justice Department breathing down his neck, interviewing disgruntled former employees of Tracker Operating Systems and subpoenaing records and assorted other company paperwork. That's why he'd come to Mexico—to get away, to think, to plan. And then Marnie LaRue had sashayed into his life, listening to the same Motown music he preferred and muddling up his brain with her mile-long legs and lush sweep of lashes.

He'd be damned if he could get a bead on her. She was after something, had to be. But he still couldn't figure out what. A job? An interview? A ring?

Still, he'd give her this: she certainly had a different approach than the others.

He rubbed his sore jaw and, though he berated himself for it, admired the view as she stalked away.

They steered clear of each other for the better part of the day, which was easy to do since Marnie spent most of it in town. She called her parents and talked to her son, who, as she'd suspected, had already renegotiated his bedtime and met his candy quota for the month.

The man from whom Marnie had rented the house apologized for the lack of electricity, but confirmed what she had suspected: it might well stay out for the remainder of her visit. So she purchased bottled water, some wine and more ice for the small cooler she'd brought with her from her parents' house, determined to make the best of her brief holiday.

This time the man's niece, who worked at a resort in Los Cabos, was in town to do the translating. She spoke English easily, with the side benefit of a lovely accent that lent a lyrical quality to even the most mundane words.

"My uncle wants to know if you've met the other American?" she asked.

"Oh, yeah, I've met J.T."

A few young women sitting at one of the tables in the café giggled at the mention of his name.

"Ignore them," Marisa suggested. "All of the women around here have a little—how do you say?—crush on J.T."

"He's something, all right. I met him in here first, as a matter of fact, and we've run in to each other a couple of times since then. He still has electricity," Marnie said. "Why is that?"

"Generator," Marisa replied.

Her curiosity got the better of her. "Does he live here? Year-round, I mean."

"Not year-round, no. He's American, like you. He just comes for visits."

"But does he own that place?"

"Yes. He has been coming to La Playa de la Pisada for a couple of years. Very mysterious." She lowered her voice to a conspiratorial whisper. "Some say he is crazy."

"I can vouch for that," Marnie muttered.

"Others say he is a drug dealer."

"Drug dealer?"

Marnie couldn't picture that. The guy was a royal pain in the fanny, but he didn't seem like some sort of sleazy lawbreaker despite that wad of bills he carried. He was as suspicious as all get out, but would a drug dealer wade into the ocean intent on saving the life of someone he didn't even like?

"*Si.* Me, I do not believe it. I think he is a booty hunter."

"A wh-what?" Marnie sputtered.

"Booty hunter," Marisa replied sincerely.

"Lot's of men are," Marnie said on a laugh. "But I'm thinking you mean *bounty* hunter."

"Ah, that is the word. *Si.*"

"What makes people think he's a bounty hunter?" Marnie asked, intrigued.

The other woman shrugged, but leaned in closer.

"He seems to do a lot of watching and driving. And a friend of my cousin has been inside his house. He hires her from time to time to come in and clean. She says he has all sorts of impressive equipment and computers. And last week, just after he arrived, she was there freshening up the sheets when she heard him on the telephone talking to somebody about justice and being a tracker."

Bounty hunter? Marnie thought it seemed far-fetched. But he fit the image she'd always had in her head when it came to the people who went after bail jumpers: Big, brawny, a little on the rogue side. And might that explain why he was so curious about who sent her? Did he think she was up to no good? Or, did he think she was out to collar some criminal before he did?

Marnie LaRue, bail bond agent. The very thought had her smiling. Then she set aside her mirth. The mysterious J.T. was none of her concern, she decided and headed back to her heavenly slice of golden beach, listening to Aretha's soulful voice all the way.

When evening rolled around again, Marnie still did not have electricity. She glanced down the beach at the light already visible through the windows of J.T.'s abode. She really didn't want to spend another night in the dark with nothing to eat but charred hotdogs. She didn't particularly like the man, but she could tolerate him if it meant at some point she could ask to borrow his shower. And, after her conversation in town with Marisa, she had to admit she was even more intrigued by him. She decided she would go over, act nice and see if that got her foot far enough in the door to feel the brisk spray from a showerhead before she had to leave.

In the meantime, she would ignore the fact that J.T. had her hormones on full alert. It was a fluke, pure and simple. It had to be since the last time she'd felt this way, she'd been seventeen and head-over-heels smitten with Hal LaRue.

Marnie smiled absently, thinking about those golden days of the not so distant past when she had shamelessly wheedled and maneuvered in order to get what she most wanted.

And what she had most wanted was Hal.

She'd been the one to actually ask him out for their first date. She'd been a senior in high school at the time and she figured she'd waited long enough for him to get around to it. She'd set her sights on him when they were both juniors. She'd been a cheerleader, the homecoming queen. He'd been captain of the...chess club.

Okay, so most people hadn't understood the attraction. But Marnie had found his brains as sexy as the way they were packaged: beneath tidy blond hair and behind wire-rimmed glasses that drew attention to a pair of serious, soulful dark eyes.

His physique leaned more wiry than brawny, which made sense since he ran cross country, but he could quote Shakespeare! None of the other boys Marnie dated would have known Hamlet from a ham sandwich, but Hal—Mr. Valedictorian, Mr. Quiz Bowl captain and a member of the debate team—had.

Someone with his brains could have gone anywhere, done anything. But he'd graduated from high school, attended Michigan Technological Institute in nearby Houghton for a while, and then he'd come back to tiny Chance Harbor on Lake Superior's shore, three semesters shy of obtaining his degree.

"I don't want to move to some unfamiliar city and work at some impersonal company," he'd told her in that simple, straightforward manner of his. "Odds are good that's exactly what I'll wind up doing. Mechanical engineers aren't in high demand in Chance Harbor. But this is where I want to live and raise a family." He'd waited a heartbeat before adding, "With you."

Marnie sighed now, remembering with bittersweet clarity the way their life had unfolded perfectly according to plan—at first.

Hal had gotten a job with the county and bought a small house within a stone's throw of the biggest of the Great Lakes. He'd worked his way up to a department head by the time he finally asked her to marry him. Marnie had been twenty-seven by then and she'd said yes without hesitation. Slow, plodding Hal. For a while there, she'd thought she might have to pop the question herself.

In the end, they had only celebrated two wedding anniversaries before he'd died. And now she'd marked three anniversaries without him.

She glanced across the beach again, thinking about J.T. and the inappropriate tingle of attraction she'd felt when she'd first met him. What was it about him that called to her? He had that golden god thing going for him, sure, but even if she were in the market for a man, which she most certainly was not, Marnie wanted someone who was capable of stimulating conversation as well as mind-blowing sex. She'd had both with Hal. She'd never settle for less.

The memories, bittersweet and poignant, almost stopped her from leaving the house. As it was, she stepped back inside, telling herself it was just to get a sweater to pull over her T-shirt and shorts since it had grown chilly out as daylight waned.

A year ago, Marnie would have spent the remainder of the evening wallowing in unhappy thoughts peppered with what-ifs and if-onlys. Tonight, determination had her shrugging into the sweater, grabbing a bag of potato chips she'd brought from Arizona and the bottle of wine she bought earlier that day, and walking out the door. She was alive. She needed to act that way, not only for herself, but also for Noah.

Besides, it was really all about the possibility of a shower and nothing more, she told herself, intent on ignoring that fluky flutter in her belly.

Still, she didn't miss the irony that as she crossed the stretch of beach she was quite literally walking out of the darkness and toward the light.

CHAPTER THREE

J.T. was scowling when he opened his door. He wore a long-sleeved lightweight pullover with a discreet designer insignia embroidered on the front and a pair of faded jeans in deference to the temperature dip. But his feet, tanned and the tops sprinkled with golden hair, were bare.

He leaned against the jamb and crossed his arms. "Come to apologize?"

Marnie had, thinking that might be the best way to wheedle a shower out of him, but she would be damned if she was going to now and have him believe she had somehow been shamed into it.

"Peace offering," she said instead, holding out the chips and wine.

He didn't invite her inside. He came out instead and closed the door firmly behind him before she could glimpse much of the interior. Still, she wondered, had those countertops been made of granite or marble? His place definitely was a huge step up from hers and Marisa had said he owned it.

"Are you coming?"

She watched one sandy eyebrow lift, as if he were daring her to comment or ask a question. She swallowed both.

"Lead the way," she said instead.

A small wicker table and chairs took up most of a small patio on the side of the house that faced the ocean. J.T. accepted her gifts and headed toward it, turning his chair so that he was looking at the water when he sat.

The sun had almost set. It was but an orange glow melting onto the ocean's relatively calm surface. And if not for the light that spilled from between the blind slats of the window behind him, Marnie might not have been able to make out his expression. But she could. His jaw was firmly clenched, as if her presence irritated him. He didn't exactly invite her to sit and join him, but she did anyway.

"So, how long are you down here for?" she asked conversationally as she settled into her chair. She could hear her mother's voice in her ear: A polite host or guest doesn't monopolize the conversation but tries to get others to talk about themselves.

Clearly J.T.'s mother had made no admonition. At his glare, Marnie sighed.

"Oh, that's right. You can ask questions, but apparently I'm not allowed to. I've got to tell you, J.T., given your attitude, it's really no wonder that you vacation alone."

If he was insulted, it didn't show. "And what's your reason?"

"I'm not vacationing."

She thought about the morning spent lazing on the beach and the afternoon spent poking through the little shops in town, dickering with the locals over trinkets and a rather sparse assortment of souvenirs to take home.

"Not really," she amended.

"Ah."

She watched his eyes narrow. Why was the man so prickly, so suspicious all the time? And was the reason something she should be nervous about? The conversation with Marisa came to mind again. So, some of the locals thought the man might be a drug dealer? But Marnie's instincts had rarely failed her, and she trusted them this time. A drug dealer he was not. He had some money. That much was clear from that glimpse into his house—vacation home no less—and his quality clothing.

For instance, the designer logo on the shirt he wore told her that despite the garment's casual cut, it commanded a pretty formidable price for what amounted to a long-sleeved T-shirt.

"So, why are you here?" he asked for what seemed like the millionth time.

"I've already told you that I'm just on the Baja Peninsula to get away."

"Because life in bustling Chance Harbor is so hectic?"

It didn't dawn on her to wonder how he knew that Chance Harbor was anything but bustling. Instead she thought about her day-in, day-out struggle to eke out a living while single-handedly raising her son. She wanted more than that for Noah. Once upon a time, she'd wanted more than that for herself.

"Something like that."

Because her tone had turned melancholy, she forced a smile to her lips and, determined to keep the conversation light, she asked, "Do you have glasses or are we going to drink that wine straight from the bottle?"

J.T. studied her in the meager light. He didn't want to get glasses. Getting glasses would mean they would be sharing more time together and he had already decided that wouldn't be a good idea. There was some-

thing about this woman that told him to turn
tail and run. Something about her was dangerous. Even if for just a moment she had seemed
almost sad, vulnerable.

She crossed her shapely legs, letting one
sandal dangle flirtatiously from her left foot.
Despite the gathering dark, he knew that her
toenails were painted a fiery red.

Vulnerable? No way. She was dangerous.
Very, very dangerous.

When he failed to answer her question, she
merely shrugged and, without another word,
tore open the bag of chips. She scooped out a
handful for herself before turning the bag toward him. He resisted the offer, determined to
resist the woman as well.

After munching on the chips, she brushed
her hands together and brought her feet up
onto the chair seat. Wrapping her arms around
her legs, she rested her chin on her knees and
said, "If you drive up the west side of the
Keewenau—it's a peninsula in Michigan's

Upper Peninsula—you can see sunsets like the ones here on Superior."

"It's a lake," he said dryly. "You can't compare a sunset on the ocean to a sunset on a lake."

"It's not *a* lake. It's a *Great* Lake," she countered.

"So?"

She shook her head in apparent dismay.

"You know, a few years back some U.S. senator got the bright idea to reclassify Lake Champlain in Vermont as a Great Lake. Something to do with funding of some sort for some project or another."

She waved her hand in a dismissive gesture.

"Well, folks in Michigan got a little hot about it, I can tell you. We take our Great Lakes pretty seriously."

"So I gather," he replied, intrigued despite himself. This wasn't the usual conversation he found himself engaged in while sitting in the semidark with a beautiful woman.

"Newspaper columnists and assorted pundits—"

"Pundits?"

"The folks who get paid to offer supposedly informed opinions."

"I know what the word means."

"Ah." Curved eyebrows inched up. "Just shocked that I do, hmm?"

He grimaced. "I've insulted you. Sorry."

But she merely shrugged. "I'm not blond, but I get a lot of that. Anyway, back to my story. The pundits came up with all sorts of ways to define what constitutes a Great Lake. They made up top ten lists, that sort of thing. Do you want to hear my favorite?"

"By all means."

"You know it's a Great Lake if you can't see across it." She turned and smiled brightly in the dim light. "Just like the ocean."

He didn't say anything for a moment. Then he got up and walked to the door with the wine bottle in his hand.

"Calling it a night?" she asked.

He stood for a moment with his back to her. He could go inside, he knew, close the door and pass an evening in quiet comfort before his state-of-the-art entertainment center or his equally high-tech computer, tinkering with some experimental software he was still perfecting.

But when he turned the knob and stepped inside, the words he left her with were: "Just going to open the wine."

When he came back out, he lit a few of the tiki torches that surrounded the patio. The move was practical given how dark it had become, but it also made the patio, not to mention their conversation, seem more intimate.

A couple of hours later they had polished off more than half the bottle of wine. The merlot wasn't up to J.T.'s usual standards. This bottle probably cost less than ten dollars, whereas the hand-blown goblets they drank it out of ran more than five times that, each. And yet he couldn't remember when he had enjoyed a vintage more.

He didn't want to admit it was Marnie's company that had bumped the dry red up several notches in his estimation. He let her dominate the conversation—not that he really had any choice in the matter. But he didn't find himself bored by her ongoing commentary. She was an interesting conversationalist. Far more went on inside that gorgeous head than he knew most people gave her credit for when they first met her. That applied to him as well.

Yet, as the evening wore on, he also realized he didn't know anything more about Marnie LaRue than he had that morning. She was a regular pro at saying a lot without really telling him anything substantial or revealing. Even the wine hadn't loosened her tongue enough that she'd confided the real reason for her trip to Mexico.

He topped off her glass with the remainder of the wine and hoped for the best.

Then he nearly choked when she said, "So, are you a drug dealer or a bounty hunter?"

"Excuse me?"

"A drug dealer or a bounty hunter? That's the speculation of the locals given your nice little setup here. Or just plain crazy. My money's on the third, but I could see the second. Not the first, though."

"Oh?"

"I figure a drug dealer would have let me drown."

So, he had apparently become the topic of local gossip. That was something he hoped to avoid unless he wanted this little slice of isolation to become crowded with media and others seeking an audience with Jonathan Thomas Lundy. But J.T. found himself too intrigued by Marnie's comments to worry over that fact right now.

"So, if I were a drug dealer, I would have let you drown. But not if I were a bounty hunter?"

"You'd be in the business of upholding the law, even if your methods might be somewhat unorthodox." When he raised an eyebrow, she said, "I used to watch a lot of cable."

"What if I'm just crazy?"

She merely shrugged. "Never said you weren't."

"Touché."

The conversation almost had him convinced she wasn't a reporter. Surely by now she would have tried to sniff out more information on the Justice Department's action. That left two other possibilities and he was leaning toward conniving woman when she said, "Your house seems a little nicer than the one I'm renting. And I notice you still have electricity."

This conversation was heading somewhere, he thought, as he replied slowly, "Yes, I do."

"And your shower, would the water be hot and clear or, say, brown and cold?"

"Hot and clear. I just took a really long one a couple of hours ago. Felt wonderful."

"I'll bet." She made a little humming noise in the back of her throat. "You know, the man I rented my place from said it could be days before my power is restored and I'm leaving on Monday. Even if it does come back on before then, so that I can take a hot shower, the odds are good that my water will still be rusty."

"A pity."

"Isn't it? I was wondering if you…might know a place where I could get a shower."

"Perhaps, but it will cost you." The words were out before he could think better of them.

"And the price?"

Her tone was careful rather than flirtatious, but a few different scenarios sprang into J.T.'s mind anyway, not one of them clean enough for a PG-rating. He cleared his throat, wishing he could clear his head as well. But the prurient thoughts seemed to lodge themselves front and center in his brain like pesky burrs.

"Answer a question for me."

"Should have guessed," she muttered. But then she conceded with a smile. "For a long, hot shower, my life is an open book. Ask away."

He thought for a moment, trying to decide what he most wanted to know. More likely she would take pleasure in reminding him that he had only stipulated that she answer *a* question, singular, in trade for shower privileges. She struck him as a woman who paid close attention even when she seemed distracted or relaxed.

"The suspense is killing me," she teased when he remained silent.

"Just trying to figure out what it is that I most want to know."

"They're real," she deadpanned and J.T. couldn't help himself, he laughed out loud.

"That wasn't what I was going to ask. In

fact, it never even crossed my mind that they might be anything other than authentic." He waggled his eyebrows. "Of course, there is one sure method to prove that point beyond a shadow of a doubt."

Her expression remained bland. "In your dreams, *amigo*."

And he had a feeling that was exactly what would be on his mind when he finally drifted off to sleep that night.

"There's a time limit on the question and you're fast approaching it. After that you forfeit the right to ask and I get to take a shower anyway."

"Says who? It's not like this is *Jeopardy*."

But all she said was, "Tick, tick, tick."

"Are you married?" he blurted out at last.

The question hung in the cool air between them. J.T. wondered what had possessed him to ask it. What did it matter if she was taken? Much better questions were: Are you after something? Do you know who I really am?

Still, he realized he had been holding his breath when she finally answered.

"No. I have no husband."

She stood and began to walk back to her place.

He hadn't wanted Marnie there when she arrived earlier in the evening and yet he didn't want her to leave now. He was bored, that was all. That was the only reason he wanted her to stay. Many adjectives came mind to describe Marnie LaRue, but boring was not one of them.

"I didn't mean to make you uncomfortable," J.T. called after her.

She stopped and turned back toward him, but she was far enough from the light of the torches now that he could no longer see her face.

"You didn't."

"Then why are you leaving?"

"Just going to get my stuff. I can't take a

shower without my Loufa, bath gel, shampoo, conditioner and moisturizing lotion. Be right back."

As good as her word, Marnie tapped at his door five minutes later smiling brightly and toting a toiletry bag the size of his carry-on luggage.

He staggered back a step in surprise and she took the opportunity to breeze inside, setting down the wheeled case, which she then rolled right over his toes.

"I did say just a shower, right?" He pointed to the bag. "You look like you're planning to move in."

"It's just a few essentials," she told him, blinking slowly and looking as innocent as a newborn baby. "I haven't had a chance to pamper myself in a while, so I thought I'd go all out."

"The hot water heater only holds fifty gallons. That going to be enough?" He was trying for sarcasm, but she merely lifted an eyebrow.

"I guess I'll have to make do."

And it terrified J.T. that he had no idea if she was teasing.

"Follow me."

He watched her eyes widen marginally as he led her to the master bath through the well-appointed interior of his outwardly humble home. She didn't say a word for most of the way, but he knew that if Marnie LaRue had been curious about who he was and what he was doing in La Playa de la Pisada before, she was doubly so now.

The home's only bathroom could be entered from either the living room or the master bedroom. She broke the silence as they passed a row of framed and matted black and white photographs on the wall.

"Is that you?"

There were five shots in all, taken from the top of a ski slope in Aspen, Colorado. Even in black and white, they offered a breathtaking view. J.T. appeared in profile in only one of the shots, the last in the five arranged horizontally on the wall.

"Yes."

"I'm no expert, but the photographer is very talented."

"She is that," he said, smiling absently, as he thought about his younger sister, Anne. And then he decided it best to change the subject.

"Fresh towels and washcloths are in the linen closet," he said, pointing to a slim, distressed wood cabinet that ran from floor to the ceiling.

"Thanks." She put her case on the countertop, toed off her sandals and watched him with those slow-blinking eyes. It took J.T. a moment to realize she was waiting for him to leave.

"Oh, uh, I'll just…" he began, taking a step backward. The door had closed a quarter of the way, and the slim edge caught him in the back as he retreated.

Marnie smiled, enjoying the fact that big, hulking J.T. seemed to have been thrown off balance. Never one to pass up an opportunity, she walked toward him, peeling off her sweater and then untucking the hem of her T-shirt as she came. It had been a long time since she'd played this kind of cat and mouse game with a member of the opposite sex, but she hadn't lost her touch she decided smugly when she saw his Adam's apple bob.

As the *coup de grace,* she snagged the hem of her shirt with both hands and began to work it up. Slowly. She knew a moment of pure feminine power that J.T.'s gaze never strayed from the incremental progress.

He may not be sure he likes me, and we may have started off on the wrong foot, but there's no mistaking that he's interested.

When the shirt hem began to flirt with the lace edging on the underside of her bra, J.T.

exhaled sharply and Marnie took devilish delight in stretching out her right leg and using
her foot to shove the door closed in his face.

"Be out in a bit," she called sweetly.

"Take your time. *Please.*"

And she did. For the next hour, J.T. heard
her in the bathroom, making do, as she'd
called it. And, God help him, he couldn't get
his mind off her, that flirty little pseudo strip-
tease she'd managed or how she would look
standing in the middle of his shower, which,
conveniently, was big enough for two. The
stall was surrounded in mossy green marble
he'd had shipped in special from Italy, with
dual chrome heads that pumped pulsating
streams of water from opposing vantage
points. He pictured Marnie standing between
them, water streaming over her curves in a
sensuous cascade.

After twenty minutes of mental torture and
three hastily gulped glasses of ice water, he retreated to the den tucked just off the living

room, deciding to put as much distance as possible between him and the sound of Marnie alternately humming and singing a medley of Motown tunes. He couldn't fault her taste in music, he thought wryly, even if she did have a voice that was meant *only* for the shower.

In the den, he booted up his computer and typed in his password. He had some files he needed to review and he might as well check his e-mail, anything to keep his mind off his beguiling houseguest.

He was in the middle of going through a report from one of his senior vice presidents when he heard the bathroom door open. A moment later, Marnie appeared in the den, bringing the feminine scent of perfumed lotion with her. Hastily he signed off and then clicked closed the half dozen windows he had open on his computer screen.

"Working?" she asked.

She had one of his thick white towels

wrapped turban style around her head and wore a pair of loose drawstring capris with a matching navy pullover. Nothing about the outfit was overtly sexy, but the whole package that made up Marnie LaRue was infinitely so.

"Can't let the bad guys get away now, can we?"

He meant it to be teasing, but realized she took him seriously when she replied, "Must be an interesting line of work, being a bounty hunter."

"All work has its ups and downs." He shrugged, deciding there was nothing wrong with being vague or employing a little subterfuge. They were, basic sexual attraction and the use of his shower notwithstanding, barely more than acquaintances.

"And dangerous. Ever been shot at?"

He thought about his competitors and what he considered their sympathizers at the Justice Department.

"I'm sure there are plenty of people who

would like to get a round or two off at my expense, but I've been lucky so far."

Her face had clouded.

"My brother was shot several years ago."

Instantly he regretted his flippant tone. "I'm sorry. Is he…okay?"

"Fine now, and thankfully he's given up investigative work, found himself a good woman and a new, less risky career path, so I don't have to worry about him anymore."

She tugged the towel off her head, laid it over the back of the desk chair and began to finger-comb her hair.

"Why do people take such risks?" she asked.

For some reason he didn't think she was talking about her brother now, and though he couldn't pinpoint why, her expression had turned sad and there was that vulnerability he had glimpsed earlier in the evening.

He shrugged. "What's the saying? 'Nothing ventured, nothing gained.'"

"You can turn that saying around, you know. 'Nothing ventured, nothing lost.'"

He thought about Terri, about the bickering and finally the betrayal that had led up to their messy court battle and the ugly he-said, she-said testimony that was duly reported in the media. Marnie had a point. He certainly regretted having taken that chance.

Still, his experience in business convinced him of the need to take risks—acceptable ones where he weighed ahead of time what he could afford to lose. After all, if not for that first big gamble, in which he'd plunked every last bit of his savings and whatever else a bank had been willing to loan him, Tracker Operating Systems would still be a pipedream and not one of the biggest software developers and manufacturers in the world.

He couldn't tell her all that, though. Instead he said, "Life's a little more interesting when it has an edge."

She shrugged.

"I don't agree, but I'm afraid I'm too tired to argue the point right now."

As if to punctuate her words, she yawned before going to gather her things. J.T. followed her to the door, glad she was finally leaving and yet sorry to see her go. The evening had passed quickly and enjoyably in her company.

"Thank you for the use of your shower."

"You're welcome."

She tilted her head to one side. "I was hoping you were going to say 'any time.' Even if my power comes back on before I leave Monday and the water turns crystal clear, I'm afraid your shower has spoiled me."

Just as she had spoiled the shower for him. J.T. doubted he would ever take another one in that bathroom without thinking of her.

"Felt that good, huh?"

"Incredible."

Her slow smile had his mouth going dry. And suddenly he had to know: How would she feel in his arms? What would she taste like if he kissed her?

Marnie didn't back away when he reached for her. She molded against him, resting her hands on his shoulders, although those dark eyes regarded him warily. When their mouths met, he thought he heard her sigh. And he knew he wanted to—the relief, the release of tension, seemed that great.

The kiss began hungry and only got more so when he changed the angle and she opened up to him. Marnie wasn't shy, but she was greedy. No, not greedy, he amended. She gave back as much as she took. Hungry, that's what she was. Hot. J.T. felt consumed by the heat and he was only too happy to burn.

When the kiss ended, it was his turn to say, "Incredible."

Marnie nodded, looking somewhat surprised, maybe even a little shaken.

"It was nice, wasn't it?"

"Nice? Let's try that again and see if you can come up with a better adjective."

But she backed away this time.

"I don't think your ego needs any more feeding at this point."

She'd been the one to end the kiss, as he figured she would be, since that would give her the upper hand. They'd known each other for only a couple of days and he'd already figured that much out about her. She wanted to be in control.

Still, he liked knowing he could shake her up, and the way her breath still shuddered in and out of her lungs told J.T. that he had, no matter how nonchalant Marnie was now trying to act.

"I had a *nice* time tonight," she said, taking delight in stressing the word. "Maybe I'll see you on the beach tomorrow morning."

"Is that an invitation?"

Her lips bowed into a sultry smile. "Let's say around nine."

"I'll be there."

"And I'll look forward to it."

Just when he was beginning to feel smug, she added, "Bring an extra cup of Starbucks this time. Black for me, too. The way God intended a good cup of coffee to be."

She was so shameless about using him that J.T. had to grin. At least all she appeared to be after—for the moment anyway—was a hot shower and a steaming cup of French roast. He'd rarely gotten off that cheaply when it came to members of the opposite sex.

As he opened the door for her, he said, "I'll walk you back. Wouldn't want you to get lost in the dark."

He reached for her bag, but she shook her head.

"Thanks, but no need. I never lose my way."

Then, pulling the trusty flashlight from the front pocket of her case, she was on her way, following the beam as it danced across the beach.

CHAPTER FOUR

I NEVER lose my way.

Marnie had told J.T. that the night before, and yet she knew it wasn't quite true. She'd stumbled plenty after that kiss, barely knowing right from left, up from down, back from front.

Oh, she'd pretended to act unmoved, even as her knees had turned liquid and her body had turned traitor. But the fact of the matter remained, she'd wanted J.T.

Right then, right there in his hard-surfaced kitchen, she had wanted him.

He was the first man she'd kissed, let alone fantasized about doing much more with, since Hal. She thought she should feel guilty about that. She'd loved her husband. But guilt, she was practical enough to realize, wouldn't bring him back or undo the past. So, the only thing Marnie felt was dizzying sexual attraction and even a bit of smug satisfaction that she wasn't the only one who'd been left dazed and breathless.

The minutes of her stay in La Playa de la Pisada were ticking steadily away, and yet as she laid in bed on this Sunday morning— something she hadn't done in too many Sundays to count—she found she didn't want to leave.

She felt reinvigorated. She missed her son and God knew she missed the convenience of electricity and hot running water, but she was in no hurry to return to either her parents' well-meaning hovering or her staid life minding the tap and managing the business end of the Lighthouse Tavern while her brother was out of town.

Sure, this thing with J.T.—assuming it hadn't

already run its course—would be fleeting, and not just because she couldn't stay in La Playa de la Pisada forever. Marnie was a careful woman, even more so now that she had a son to raise by herself. The man was a bounty hunter—if that wasn't risk personified, what was? And besides, what did the pair of them have in common beyond an appreciation for Motown music and a taste for merlot?

Of course, it didn't *have* to mean anything. She felt very *Sex and the City*-ish as she lay in bed, one hand flung negligently over her head, the other plucking at the thin fabric of her camisole, and mulled over the possibility of a brief, albeit mutually satisfying, fling. What man wouldn't want that? No strings, no commitment. Just sex. Lots and lots of glorious sex.

At the knock on her door, Marnie bolted upright. Then she heard J.T.'s voice calling out her name. Could the man read her mind? She fanned her heated face and hoped not.

"I'm…just a minute."

She scrambled for clothes, hastily pulling on a sweater and shorts. She paused in the bathroom to run a comb through her hair and splash some bottled water on her face. Then, satisfied that she no longer looked flustered or aroused, she went to open the door.

Thoughts of sex might have had her unsettled, but she forgot all about feeling self-conscious when she spied J.T. Her gaze lingered for only a moment on his handsome face, the lower half of which was bristled with twenty-four hours' worth of beard and sported a sexy half grin. Then her gaze veered to the extra mug of steaming coffee he held in his hand.

"I didn't see you on the beach," he said as his gaze took a meandering tour of her features. "You did say nine?"

"Yes, I did. You're very punctual."

"Among other things," he agreed, holding out the cup.

She snatched it from his fingers and drank

greedily. A quarter of the mug's contents was gone before she came up for air and then sighed deeply.

"Mmm. You're a saint."

"A saint?" He raised one sandy eyebrow at that assessment and something decidedly wicked flickered in his blue eyes. "Don't canonize me yet. I could burn in hell for what I'm thinking at the moment."

Marnie had been about to invite him inside, but she thought better of it now. She knew exactly the kinds of thoughts he was entertaining, as she had entertained them herself mere minutes before. But she wasn't the sort to leap before looking, no matter how cozy the bed looked at this point.

"Let's go for a walk," she said, grabbing her sunglasses and a small disposable camera from the counter near the door. Then she brushed passed him, waiting outside for him to follow her.

He turned on a sigh.

"Sure. That's what I had in mind," J.T. mumbled.

The morning was glorious, the sky as blue and calm as the ocean. The only clouds that marred its perfection looked as if they had been brushed there with a few strokes from a master painter. For the next hour, they combed the beach, stopping at this rock outcropping and that one so Marnie could snap photographs.

"Smile." Marnie turned the camera in J.T.'s direction and he quickly whirled away.

"Well, I think I managed a nice shot of the back of your head," she said. "When I said smile, I meant, smile at *me*."

"Sorry. I don't like my picture taken."

"Camera shy?" Then she said, "Oh, I get it. Your line of work. Probably not a good idea to have your photograph out there."

"Yeah."

"It's not like I'd sell it," she teased.

But J.T. didn't laugh.

Even if Marnie had no idea who he was now, he knew better than most that even a simple snapshot could wind up gracing the cover of a tabloid when or if she figured out his real identity and decided to cash in on her association.

He thought he could trust her at this point, but he wasn't a man to tempt fate. He'd done that before, with disastrous consequences. He was still dealing with the fallout of his ex-wife's tell-all—although not necessarily *tell-all-the-truth*—book of the year before. The three-hundred-and-fifty-page bestseller had included three-dozen photos from the halcyon days of their marriage, including a couple of rather risqué ones that he'd come to regret, and J.T. had vowed never to expose himself, literally or figuratively, in that way again.

"Let me take your picture," he suggested as a way of changing the subject.

Marnie happily obliged him. She leaned up against some rocks with her hips cocked, one long leg bent out to the side, head turned slightly and angled down, and ripe mouth pouting like a lingerie model would. She blinked slowly with her molasses eyes and coherent thought fled. But then she quit the siren pose, laughed and made a face at J.T. And that was the one he was sure he had captured on film.

He didn't know why, but it surprised him that she could be silly. Women who looked like her didn't tend to act goofy or outrageous in this way, at least not in his experience. Oddly enough, he considered it one of her most attractive qualities, right up there with her slow-blinking eyes and sinewy limbs.

"Look at this," Marnie said a few minutes later as she bent down to retrieve a shell. She was a couple of steps ahead of him and the view her posture afforded J.T. made him think of another one of her qualities he found particularly pleasing.

"I'm looking," he murmured.

"It's pretty, eh?"

"I notice you say that a lot."

"That things are pretty?"

"No, the 'eh' part."

She laughed outright. "It's the Yooper in me coming out, I'm afraid."

"Yooper?"

"As in U.P." When he only frowned, she said in her most instructional voice, "It stands for Upper Peninsula. Michigan is made up of two peninsulas. The one that's shaped like a mitten is the lower one." She held out her hands to demonstrate. "And the one that some folks say looks like a running rabbit—although, myself, I think that's a bit of a stretch—is referred to as the upper one."

"And the people there are Yoopers?"

"Who says you're slow?" she teased.

"What's in the U.P.? I mean, I'm not familiar with it. What's the area known for?"

She shrugged. "Hunting, fishing…fudge and pasties. Lots of folks come for the scenery, too, of course. The Pictured Rocks National Shoreline, old copper mines, Tahquamenon Falls. And we even have mountains, the Porcupines, which are really more like hills compared to the Rockies or the ones here on the Baja, but they offer a nice view of things. Where I live, it's pretty and peaceful, but a little remote. Not a shopping mall in sight," she said on a wistful sigh.

"You don't seem like a small-town girl."

Her eyes narrowed. "I think I might be flattered, but I suppose I should ask, what do you think small-town girls are like?"

"I just wouldn't expect them to be as fashionable as you: Prada shoes, Kate Spade handbag."

"Oh, well, we do have magazines and a little thing called cable television," she said in her best hillbilly impersonation. Then she confided, "The shoes are a knockoff, but the bag's the real thing. My sister-in-law knows my weakness and gave it to me for my birthday last year."

"And you would have turned how old then?"

"Age is relative."

"How's that?"

"Because only my relatives know my age." She grinned and then arched an eyebrow. "Getting back to Prada and Kate Spade, I wouldn't expect a bounty hunter to recognize designer labels, although I notice you favor a few of them yourself."

"I guess we're both full of surprises."

"Full of something," she replied.

For no reason he could fathom, he heard himself say, "My education in women's fashion came courtesy of my wife. Ex-wife now."

J.T. wasn't the sort to volunteer information about his private life to those close to him, let alone to a virtual stranger. But then that kiss had made Marnie seem a lot less like someone he'd met mere days ago. Maybe it was because unlike almost everyone in his life,

Marnie treated J.T. like a normal person. She wasn't afraid to tease him or put him in his place. It was becoming clear that she didn't see dollar signs or a job promotion when she looked at him, so she could afford to be blunt.

"Ah. A lot of things about you make perfect sense now," she said.

Yes, very blunt.

"Such as?"

"Are you forgetting the first couple of times we met? You don't trust women."

"I don't trust many people," he replied and realized it was true.

He had a net worth in the billions and owned and operated one of the most innovative and profitable software companies on the planet. He attracted people—men and women—like a magnet, but he knew most of these "friends" and "supporters" and "admirers" wanted, even expected, something from him.

Walking on a beach in Mexico with Marnie, J.T. realized this was the first time in a long time that he'd simply been J.T. with no impressive title before his name, no list of credentials streaming after it.

"How long were you married?"

He grimaced. "Too long."

"Any children?"

"No, thank God."

"Don't you like children?"

"I like them fine, but under the circumstances I'm grateful there were none. They would have wound up casualties, just one more thing to fight over in court."

She kicked at the sand as she walked. "Think you'll ever do it again?"

"Get married? Hell, no." Recalling the courtroom drama, mountain of legal fees and nasty headlines he'd endured, J.T. snorted. "I'd rather be skinned alive. In fact, I think I was."

She slanted one of those slow-blinking looks his way. "Oh, I don't know. Your skin looks pretty intact to me."

"What are you doing tonight?"

"One compliment about your skin and already you're planning an evening out? You're entirely too easy, J.T. Really, you should at least pretend to play hard to get."

"You make me regret my impulsive behavior."

But he didn't regret it, not really. He wanted to continue as the man simply known as J.T. for as long as possible. So, he asked again, "Do you have plans?"

"Is a shower included in the evening's activities?"

He thought about the vivid fantasy he'd entertained the night before. God, I hope so, he thought, stifling a groan. But he merely nodded.

"Then it's a date."

But was it a date?

Marnie wondered about that as she dressed for the evening several hours later, taking more care than usual with her appearance. She'd used J.T.'s shower, but had decided to return to her rental to get ready. She chose a thin-strapped black tank top and a lightweight black and white patterned skirt that flowed to the middle of her bare calves. Everything was new, bought in Yuma on a full-day shopping excursion that her mother had insisted Marnie needed. And Marnie, never one to pass up a visit to a mall, had agreed.

In fact, she had bought half a dozen new outfits during that outing, charging it all and telling herself she would think about how she would pay for it later.

The decision, however irresponsible, had seemed less about splurging than about living. As she'd tried on those new clothes, she'd felt a bit like a butterfly newly released from its cocoon. And she hadn't stopped with clothes. She'd purchased accessories and shoes, including the pair of black slip-ons she now wore. She'd spied them on a department store's clearance rack and hadn't been able to resist. They sported a boxy silver buckle over the open toe and heels high enough that she would have felt uncomfortably tall around most men, Hal included.

But not J.T.

The thought of him had her mind tripping to the other purchases she'd made: an assortment of lingerie to accompany each outfit, because if there was one rule Marnie lived by—or at least had when fashion and foundation garments had been front and center on her list of things to worry about—was that what a woman wore beneath her clothes was just as important as the clothes themselves.

She'd brought every last lacy bra, sheer panty and flattering camisole with her to Mexico. In fact, J.T. had already glimpsed most of them that first day when she'd baldly pawed around in her luggage when he'd dared her to find something practical.

Yes, he'd seen them. But, he hadn't seen

them *on her.* Major difference, that. She ran her hands down the front of the black tank top, over her breasts that were pushed up to a gravity-defying angle thanks to a cleverly constructed underwire contraption.

Oh, no, he hadn't seen anything. Yet.

The yet part had her taking a deep breath. Was that where this was heading? Was that what this was: A now merry widow in a merry widow kicking up her heels for the first time since the worst of her mourning had passed?

Or could it be more than that?

Marnie wasn't sure when it happened or even exactly how, but she was beginning to *like* J.T., as infuriating as she still found him to be at times.

Pot calling the kettle, she thought, but then Marnie was the first to admit she had an overpowering personality. Her brother used to tease her that the only reason Hal had married her was that Marnie had done a Mount Vesuvius on him, erupting in a dazzling display that had left the poor man entombed in ash before he'd had a chance to flee.

She'd punched him for that. But Mason wasn't far off the mark. Truth be told, she had "worn the pants" in their relationship, as the saying went. But Hal hadn't been unhappy about it and neither had she. Sure, sometimes Marnie had wanted him to be a little more outspoken and assertive, a little less malleable and content with the status quo in his life, but she'd loved him.

She wasn't consciously trying to compare the two men, but she couldn't imagine a man more different from Hal than J.T. And now they were going on a date.

Or maybe it wasn't a date.

She fiddled with her hair, trying to decide what to do with it. Perhaps she and J.T. were just two people who would be passing a companionable evening together. Like they had the night before. Two Americans sharing a bit of wine and camaraderie on foreign soil.

Until that kiss.

She pushed the memory away and reached for her brush. She'd cut her hair really short about six months after Hal's death. *Really* short. Even her sister-in-law Rose had been shocked by the spiky mess it had been until it grew out to something softer. But it had been so easy to take care of. And Rose, who had lived on the street for a time, could understand and appreciate Marnie's need for short-cuts with a baby to care for and a household to run solo.

Well, Marnie's hair was long enough now that she could scrape it all back into a pony-tail with the aid of a few well-placed pins on the sides. The look brought out her eyes, which she played up with a little more shadow on the lids than she'd worn in years. She added an extra sweep of blusher to her cheeks, which had some color already thanks to a cou-ple of days of sunshine, then she stepped back to survey the overall effect in the bathroom's small, cloudy mirror.

A stranger seemed to stare back.

And yet, not a stranger. The face was thinner now, leaner through the cheeks so that it had a more sculpted appearance. But this was the old Marnie. The one who had always taken delight in dressing up, fussing with her hair, painting her nails, dabbing on perfume, and choosing just the right earrings to go with an outfit. And this pair of dangly chandeliers was indeed perfect, she decided, turning her head from side to side so she could admire them in the mirror.

She heard J.T.'s vehicle pull up outside. Butterflies fluttered to life in her stomach as the Jeep's door slammed shut. When she was barely sixteen, Mason had teased Marnie about being a diva. Pre-Hal, she would wait upstairs in the house for a boy to arrive, and only after he'd been let inside and had cooled his heels in the living room, would she descend in dramatic fashion, rescuing him from her brother and father's obligatory grilling.

"There's nothing wrong with making them wait," she had explained to Mason at the time.

But she broke her own rule now, yanking open the door even before J.T. had a chance to raise his fist and knock.

"Hmm."

That was all he said. But she wasn't so rusty at this—whether it was a date or not—that she didn't recognize male appreciation when she heard it.

"Hello."

"You look incredible," he said.

She smiled her thanks. He looked incredible, too, in his light-colored slacks and short-sleeved button-down linen shirt. Casual elegance was the phrase that came to mind and she found herself surprised again not only by how well J.T. wore clothes, but by the kind of clothing he seemed to prefer. The man had pretty refined taste for a bounty hunter, which told her he must make a decent living doing what he did.

Danger apparently paid well. The thought was sobering, but she pushed it aside. One evening out. That's all this was. That's all it could be. She was leaving the following day.

"So, what did you have in mind?" she asked as she settled into the passenger seat and pulled the belt across her lap.

Laughter rumbled from deep in his chest. "Now there's a question I don't mind hearing from a beautiful woman."

"Ah, ah, ah. Don't get ahead of yourself," she chided, even as warmth shimmied up her spine.

"I'll try to stay in the moment." He secured his own belt and then started the engine. "There's a nice place up the coast in Ensenada where I thought we could get dinner. It's a bit of a drive, if that's okay with you. But the view's worth every mile."

"Sounds lovely."

And it was. The wind had picked up since the morning, making the waves dance white, but the horizon remained clear, promising another gorgeous sunset.

They listened to Martha Reeves and the Vandellas for part of the way, and then he flipped in a CD of Gladys Knight and the Pips' greatest hits.

"I can't tell you how glad I am you like quality music. My brother is an AC/DC fan."

J.T. groaned. "You have my sympathy," he said.

"Family vacations were hell," she said. "We drove out to the Grand Canyon when I was twelve and every time he had dibs on the radio, he was tuning in to some heavy metal station or another."

"I have a younger sister. She likes pop music and even went through a phase where she listened to rap." His lip curled in distaste. "Rap. I know plenty of folks like it, but it's hardly in the same league as the hits from Classic Motown."

"In my teens, I liked Top 40," she admitted. "Just for dancing purposes, you understand."

"Uh-huh. What happened?"

Hal had happened. He'd been the person to introduce her to Smokey Robinson and the Miracles, the Four Tops, the Temptations, Marvin Gaye and the Supremes. There'd been no going back to pop after that. Marnie could appreciate other kinds of music. She even owned a few CDs by other artists. But Motown's classic rhythm and blues remained her favorite.

"I don't know." She adjusted the folds of her skirt. "I guess I just don't dance much these days."

He stilled her hand with one of his own. Giving it a squeeze he said, "I'll see what I can do to change that."

CHAPTER FIVE

THE restaurant J.T. chose was not far from a bustling resort full of Americans and Canadians and
other English-speaking guests. Even so, he
spoke in fluent Spanish to the appreciative
waiter, who quickly brought them a bottle of
wine, a chilled chardonnay this time.

They were seated on a tiled veranda that
overlooked the ocean. The veranda was par-
tially enclosed, for which Marnie was grateful since the evening air had begun to cool.
She draped the sweater she had brought
around her shoulders and, taking a sip of her
wine, regarded her dinner companion across
the linen-covered tabletop.

"How many languages do you speak?" she asked.

"Five fluently."

"Only five?"

"I'm trying to learn a couple of others."

Some of the people she knew struggled with English. Intrigued and a little in awe, she asked, "What are they?"

"English, of course. Spanish, French, Italian—"

"Ah, fluent in the romance languages, I see," she interrupted.

He winked. "My specialty."

"I'll be the judge," she replied. "What's the fifth?"

"Japanese."

Okay, she was well past awe at this point, but she asked, "And the ones you're learning?"

"I know a little—*very little*—Chinese and some German, but not enough to order in a restaurant without being surprised at what gets brought to the table."

"Well, then I'll be thankful we're not in Berlin or Beijing," Marnie said.

From the hunky look of him, she never would have figured J.T. for the studious type, and yet no one picked up foreign languages, especially to the point of fluency, without some serious time cracking open the books or spending months abroad. It seemed an odd avocation for a bounty hunter, and she said as much.

But he only shrugged, looking slightly uncomfortable when he replied, "Learning a language never goes to waste. You never know when it might come in handy."

"Is that a reminder of our first meeting?"

"Not at all." But he was grinning. "Just a point of fact."

"Say something to me in Japanese."

He arched one sandy eyebrow. "Most women would have requested French."

"I like to be different." She sipped her wine. "I like to keep you guessing."

"Well, you're succeeding," he admitted.

He rattled off a phrase, the cadence of which was so different from English that she couldn't help but smile.

"What's it mean?"

"Uh-uh." He sipped his wine and leaned forward, his gaze reflecting the candle that flickered in the center of the table. "Translation will cost extra."

"That implies I'm in debt to you already."

"Well, you do owe me a dance."

The music had started a few minutes earlier, soft and low so as not to compete with the diners' conversations. But already a few couples had made their way onto the floor in front of the band.

J.T. scooted back his chair and then came around the small table to offer Marnie his hand. She slipped it into his grasp, for all the world feeling as if she were acquiescing to more than a mere tour of the dance floor.

He led her to it and then gently guided her around the half-moon shape, his hold on her was loose and yet sure, his steps flawless. He'd done this before. *A lot.* He was too good at it not to have. Just as he was good at languages and God only knew what else. She was beginning to realize there was much more to J.T. than what first met the eye. And that scared her. So much so that for the first time in her life, Marnie felt out of her league.

His breath stirred the wisps of hair that had escaped her ponytail. He lowered his head slightly and she felt it caress the curve of her neck, warm but full of the promise of delicious heat. She shivered.

"Cold?"

"No."

Hot. She was burning up, burning with need. She'd felt this before, and yet not quite. Something about these sensations was new, bigger.

It was an all-consuming bonfire compared to the warm glow from a hearth. It terrified her.

It thrilled her.

"Who are you?" she asked, because she wasn't sure of her own identity at that point.

He pulled back enough to look at her. His gaze was steady and determined. "I'm just a man."

Somehow, Marnie doubted that.

When the song ended, he escorted her to their table. One of his strong hands rested on the small of her back, his long fingers curving slightly around her waist. The contact was simple, gentlemanly even. It made her think sinful thoughts about the other places on her body she would like his hands to touch, explore.

At the table, he pulled out her chair and waited for her to sit.

"I'm not sure I like this," she said.

"What do you mean?"

"You don't play fair."

"This isn't a game."

"See. That's what I'm talking about." She sipped her wine. "Not fair at all."

The waiter returned then to take their orders, delaying further conversation.

"Want me to order for you?"

"I think I can handle it all on my own, thanks," she said, determined to take back some of the control she had already relinquished. "After all, this menu comes with English subtitles."

"I recommend the grilled swordfish *verde,*" J.T. said. "That is if you like cilantro."

"Have you been here before?"

"A time or two." He shrugged.

"Oh?"

His eyes twinkled mischievously when he added, "You never know where a job like mine will take you."

She ordered beef tenderloin with mango salsa.

J.T. placed his order effortlessly in Spanish

and then said something else to the waiter, who smiled broadly and nodded before glancing briefly in Marnie's direction.

After he'd gone, Marnie said, "Was it flattering?"

"What?"

"The remark you made to the waiter about me."

"You don't miss a thing, do you?"

She was the mother of a four-year-old. Of course she didn't miss a thing. She had eyes in the back of her head, or so she had convinced Noah, and hearing so well honed that she could make out the sound of the cookie jar lid being lifted even when she was standing under the shower spray.

"Well?"

"I said you were beautiful and he agreed."

"Then I am flattered."

They talked companionably as they waited for their meal, and then during it, trading bites of their dishes.

"You surprised me by ordering red meat," he told her.

"Why is that? Women do eat red meat, you know."

"It's just that where I'm from every woman is either a vegetarian or on a diet."

And where would that be? she wondered, but decided not to ask. This was a fairytale. One that would end when the sun rose again and she packed up to head home.

So Marnie said instead, "Maybe I am on a diet. Atkins, you know. You get to eat all the red meat you want."

"It would be a shame for you to lose any weight seeing as how every pound is so perfectly distributed."

"Hmm. Very smooth, J.T. Who needs a foreign language to seduce a woman when complimenting her on her weight will do the job nicely? Of course, say that with a French accent and you can do with me what you will."

"Really?"

"Probably not."

"Since that wasn't a definitive no, I have hope."

"That was my intention."

She smiled slyly, enjoying the byplay. Enjoying the delicious food and stimulating conversation almost as much as the fact that she didn't have to cut up someone else's meat or remind him not to blow bubbles in his beverage. Her mother was right, Marnie realized. She'd needed this break from responsibilities to recharge her batteries.

When they finished with their meal, J.T. ordered dessert: a chocolaty confection that should have had the word sin tucked somewhere in its name. And even though Marnie had politely refused when the waiter asked if she cared for something other than the coffee she'd requested, J.T. told the man to bring two forks.

"I'm not going to have any," she insisted, even though sharing had been her plan all along. She never actually ordered dessert when she went out to eat, but she always managed to have some.

But J.T. only smiled. "I think you will. You won't be able to resist."

Her gaze stayed on his mouth, and she remembered what it had felt like pressed against her own. Tempting, very tempting.

"Is it that good?" she murmured.

"Better."

"Then I suppose I'll have to sample it, just to see if you're right."

"You won't regret it," he said.

But she was beginning to wonder. Even as she was enjoying herself, flirting recklessly, she was beginning to question whether she would regret this entire evening once she was back in Chance Harbor, wedged again into that uncomfortable, yet comforting rut. Maybe it was not wise to sample so fleeting a sensation as this evening afforded. It might make returning to the obscure and mundane that much more difficult to accept.

Even so, a moment later she used that extra fork to cut off a sliver of the dessert. It melted in her mouth, a few dozen calories worth of heaven. She sighed her appreciation.

"Well?" He cocked one eyebrow.

"It seems you were telling the truth," she said. "This is worth every sit-up, jumping jack and leg-lift I'll have to do in the morning."

"Glad you think so." Then he leaned forward and raised a hand to her mouth. "You have a little bit right here," he said, rubbing the pad of his thumb across her bottom lip. "Got it."

"Thank y——" She wasn't able to finish when he licked the chocolate off his finger.

"Delicious," he said. Then he leaned forward again.

"Is there more?"

"Oh, yeah."

But it was his lips he used this time, kissing

her thoroughly as they sat there on the veranda.

She was at a loss for words afterward, but apparently he was not so afflicted. "Check, please," he called.

Still she took satisfaction that he had called out the words in English.

Instead of returning to his Jeep, they walked on the beach afterward. The wind had picked up enough that it could no longer be classified as a breeze, but Marnie knew this wasn't why she felt so swept away. It was because the man walking with her—an intriguing, handsome and very sexy man—was also holding her hand.

"I don't even know your last name," she said, feeling a little horrified that she had kissed him twice now and had woken up that morning considering doing much more and yet she didn't know his full name.

"Lundy," he said after a moment's hesitation. "It's Lundy."

She smiled. "J.T. Lundy."

Something about the name nibbled at her memory, but she didn't have time to dwell on it. He changed the subject by asking, "Do you like margaritas?"

"They aren't my drink of choice, but when in Mexico…" she said with a shrug.

Heading back to where the Jeep was parked, he said, "I have an idea."

They went to Hussong's, a crowded bar that J.T. told Marnie was credited by some for putting the area on the map with tourists. It was, after all, where a well-known tequila-spiked beverage had been born.

"The drink was created in 1941 and named after the daughter of the German ambassador to Mexico, or so the locals say," J.T. told her.

She held up her salt-edged glass in salute.

"Here's to Margarita," Marnie said. "She must have been something, to have a drink named after her. We've never named anything for any of the people who come into the Lighthouse Tavern."

"The Lighthouse Tavern?"

"It's a bar in Chance Harbor. My family owns it. My grandfather, Daniel Striker, started it after the Second World War. Dad took over and then passed the reins to my brother. But I'm running it these days."

"A bartender?" The information surprised him. She didn't seem the sort content to mind the tap in some tavern, even one she had a personal stake in.

"Shocked?"

"Enlightened," he corrected. "No wonder I find myself wanting to confide all sorts of secrets in you."

He said it teasingly, but to his astonishment, J.T. found he actually did.

It was late when they finally headed back to La Playa de la Pisada. Marnie was so quiet on the return trip that J.T. thought she must have fallen asleep. She had her head on the rest, tilted sideways to look out the passenger window.

But just before they reached home, she said, "I'll be leaving tomorrow."

"Yes, I know."

She straightened in her seat and glanced across the console at him. "I was thinking very seriously about sleeping with you tonight."

The bald statement surprised him, even though he had hoped that was the case. Still, he swallowed hard.

"*Was* implies you no longer are."

"No."

Was that regret in her voice? He thought so, or maybe his ego just needed to believe it was.

"What changed your mind?"

"If I said, I'm not that kind of girl, would you laugh at me?"

"No." In fact, the old-fashioned notion made him respect her all the more.

"It has to mean more than just…well, you know."

His heartbeat echoed in his ears when he asked quietly, "How do you know it wouldn't?"

She sighed, a sound weighted with disgust, but he got the feeling it wasn't directed at him.

"Because I didn't even know your last name until tonight. Because, when I leave here tomorrow, the odds are good—really good—that I'll never see you again. I'm right, aren't I, J.T.?"

For just a moment, he wanted to disagree, but that was ridiculous. Their paths would not cross again. This had one-night stand written all over it, and J.T. found it odd that he'd been considering it, too, since he wasn't a bed-hopper by any stretch of the imagination. His wealth drew plenty of candidates for a solitary night of carnal delight, but he'd always passed. He had too much to lose, and he'd long ago realized that his fortune was only part of it. After all, no dollar figure could be attached to self-respect.

"Yes."

"I'm not the promiscuous sort. I mean, sure, I rented the entire first season of *Sex and the City* on video and found it entertaining, but I'm not like those women. At all. Well, except for thinking they dress divine. And then there are the shoes. I do have a shoe fetish. But the point is, I don't go around having sex just for the fun of it." She made a face, shot him a look that dared him to laugh. "You know what I mean."

J.T. wisely hid his grin. She was babbling. Adorably.

"I didn't think you did," he said.

"I'm glad, because I think I may have been sending, well, some mixed messages where you we concerned. And that's not like me, either."

"No?"

"I'm not a tease," she said pointedly.

"No."

"So, this isn't—I mean, it *wouldn't* have been a good idea. If we had, um, rather if we *had* had…" Her voice trailed away, and though the interior of the Jeep was too dark to see her face clearly, he'd lay odds she was red as a beet. He found the contrasts in her startling and sweet. The sexy and outspoken Marnie LaRue seemed suddenly as shy as a schoolgirl and at a loss for words.

"Sex," he supplied succinctly. Then he couldn't resist. "Yes, it probably would not be a good idea to pass the next several hours in a sweaty haze."

"Several hours?"

"In a sweaty haze."

"Not a good idea," she repeated softly, but it came out sounding more like a question.

"No, definitely not."

"That's not fair." But her voice was steadier now and it held a hint of amusement.

"What?"

"Few women can resist a man who claims the sex will last hours."

"Really. So, I've just made myself irresistible?"

She laughed, robustly, and sounded more like the Marnie he'd come to know and appreciate during the past few days. "I said *few* women can resist such a man. Unfortunately for you, *amigo,* I'm one of those few women."

"Damn the luck," he replied, but he couldn't help smiling in return. Never had he found the prospect of not having sex so tantalizing.

They arrived outside her place. J.T. pulled the Jeep to a stop and shifted into park.

"Can I at least kiss you good night?"

She thought about it a moment before asking, "Do these seats recline?"

"All the way to horizontal," he said with a meaningful lift of his eyebrows.

"Ah. Better walk me to my door, then."

"Too tempting?"

"For you," she replied and got out.

They kissed on her doorstep like a couple of curious teenagers: Eager to explore, but holding back.

"Should I keep my hands to myself?" he asked, coming up for air after a few minutes of what he supposed might still be called necking.

"I told you, I'm not that kind of girl," Marnie reminded him.

"Oh."

But then she grabbed his shirt and hauled him forward for another kiss, letting her own fingers roam freely over his chest before skimming down his torso and over his hips to rest on his butt. He was pretty sure that she'd just pinched him.

"I th-thought you weren't that kind of a girl," he stammered on a ragged sigh.

"I'm not. But neither am I a nun."

"Glad to know it," he said before diving back in to see just how much of this foreplay he could stand before he went completely insane.

It turned out his threshold for unconsummated intimacy was incredibly high. They spent the better part of the next twenty-five minutes working one another into a sexually frustrated froth.

"I'm going to need a cold shower after this," he commented when they finally broke apart for good. "A very, very cold shower."

Then he regarded her in the moonlight. "You could join me. As you know, my shower stall is more than big enough to accommodate two consenting adults. We could..." He trailed kisses down her neck and over her shoulder, moving the thin straps of her shirt and bra out of the way as he did so. "Wash each other's backs," he finished.

Marnie snorted out a laugh. "Like that's all that would happen. I do still have a few working brain cells." To herself, she admitted that might be *all* she had at this point. She adjusted her clothing, pulling the straps back into place. "But there's a whole ocean out there, cool as can be. We could take a dip, work off all of this heat and energy."

"We could do that in the shower."

"No doubt."

"So?"

"No dice. The ocean. That's the only place you're going to come into contact with my wet, slippery skin. Take it or leave it."

He groaned. "That imagery is pure torture."

She grinned. "I know. That was the point."

"I don't get it. When did I lose control of this situation?"

The question was rhetorical, but Marnie answered him anyway.

"Who says you ever had it?"

"Oh, I had it," J.T. insisted. "We both know I did. You were putty in my hands at one point—I think it was when I mentioned spending a few hours in a sexual haze." He skimmed a hand skillfully down her side in a way that caused her to shiver. "That was the point. Definitely. I'm sure of it."

Never one to concede defeat, Marnie pulled her hair free from the ponytail band and tossed her head in a careless motion until dark waves of hair framed her face. The gesture was sexy and she damn well knew it.

"You might have piqued my interest with that boast of your endurance," she conceded. "But like a typical man, you overplayed your hand. Your arrogance slapped me back to my senses. I suppose I should thank you."

"And I know how."

"Forget it."

His hand was still resting on her hip and he used it to draw her forward. Nuzzling her neck, he whispered, "My mother always said cockiness would be my downfall."

"Trust me on this: Mothers are never wrong."

And, despite issuing what J.T. swore was a helpless little moan of pleasure when his tongue flicked quickly across the lobe of her ear once and then came back for a lazy second time, she stepped away from him.

"The beach. Swimming," she said, using arm motions as if she were speaking to someone slow.

And at that moment, he had to admit, he felt downright mired in her.

"I just want to go on the record as saying I disagree wholeheartedly with your method of working off energy."

"So noted."

"Perhaps it should come up for a vote?"

"It would be a tie."

"No tie-breaker?"

"No vote."

"A question then."

She folded her arms over her chest. "By all means. Ask away."

"What will you be wearing for this swim of ours?"

Marnie's eyes narrowed, but her lips

twitched when she replied, "My swimsuit, Don Juan, my swimsuit."

"I was afraid you were going to say that." And his groan was hardly manufactured for effect.

"Meet you on the beach in fifteen," Marnie told him and she looked as pleased as a cat lapping up cream when she closed the door in his face.

CHAPTER SIX

ONCE she found her flashlight and lit a few candles, it still took Marnie nearly half an hour to put on her swimsuit. Only a couple of those minutes were actually required to slip into the clever tank's spandex. The first twenty-seven were spent wondering if she'd lost her mind.

Playing with fire, that's what this was. She felt scorched already from the intense heat the mere brush of his fingers over her skin could ignite. But she didn't want the evening—or this sweet torture—to end just yet. She wasn't ready to go back to being Noah's mom and Hal's widow. To being regarded as that *Poor Marnie LaRue.* Here, tonight, she was simply

Marnie with no tragic history and none of the ardor-cooling responsibilities of motherhood.

"I thought you might have changed your mind," J.T. said when she joined him.

In her absence, he'd stoked a fire to life in a makeshift pit halfway between their two homes.

"I'm not quite ready to call it a night."

"Glad to hear that."

J.T. tossed another piece of kindling onto the fire and settled onto a blanket that was spread over the sand. He'd brought out refreshments as well, she noted, packed in a wicker hamper. The gesture was more romantic than she wanted it to be, as was the firelight. Its flickering glow bathed him in gold.

"You have a nice eye for details," she said, nodding in the direction of the basket.

He shrugged. "I try."

"Well then, you deserve an A for effort."

She had pulled a sweatshirt over the bathing suit and was glad for it given the chilly night air. Settling onto the blanket next to him she drew her legs up close to her body and held her hands out to the flames for warmth.

"That dip's going to be mighty cold, I'm thinking," J.T. said at last.

"Very."

She was shivering. In anticipation of the cold water or further contact with the sexy man next to her, she wasn't certain.

"Maybe we should make sure we're good and hot to make it worth the shock to our systems."

"Going to put another log on the fire?" she inquired innocently.

"Something along those lines, yes."

And he reached for her.

The fire crackled and a log broke apart, sending up a shower of sparks, but it was Marnie who burned, taking delight in her slow incineration. She found herself pinned beneath J.T. on the blanket, the sand providing little cushion with his weight pressed into her, but her mind didn't register discomfort, only a delicious kind of pressure building from within as well as without.

I'm going to remember this night, this night of *almost,* she told herself, enjoying the solid feel of him.

Appropriately enough, from his portable CD player, Martha Reeves & the Vandellas were singing "(Love Is Like A) Heat Wave" as Marnie helped J.T. work the sweatshirt up over her head. He tossed it aside blindly as his lips lingered on her neck. Then his mouth slid across the ridge of her collarbone and she was lost.

"Mmm." The sound vibrated from her throat, reminiscent of a cat's contented purring.

"You said it."

J.T. slipped the strap of Marnie's suit over her right shoulder, raining kisses there as well.

"I never realized before that shoulders were

an erogenous zone," Marnie whispered on a sigh.

"Neither did I."

"Maybe *Cosmopolitan* should do an article on it," she suggested, trying to keep her head even as his breath singed her already heated skin.

He moved to her left shoulder, applying the same sensual treatment. The second strap slipped low on her shoulder, tugged down by J.T.'s teeth, and right along with the strap came the top of her suit until quite a bit more than mere cleavage was exposed to the chilly night air.

"God, you're beautiful," he rasped.

This can't go any farther. The words screamed through her head, but never made it to her lips. Even so, J.T. stopped abruptly. Marnie's body was still humming with pleasure and yearning for release as he thoughtfully pulled her suit back into place, showing far more good sense than she was at the moment.

He blew out a gusty breath and settled his forehead against hers. "Better take that swim."

It was her turn to exhale sharply. "I think that's a good idea."

He stood and helped Marnie to her feet. Then he pulled off his shirt and dropped it in a heap on the blanket, after which he reached for her hand and laced his fingers through hers.

"I want to keep you close," he said and her heart tripped over in her chest, pounding erratically even after he added, "The tide can be dangerous."

They stayed near the shore and their swim was brief, just long enough to let the chilly water douse the last of their ardor. In its place, companionship settled, playfulness even when she used her hand to splash water in his direction.

They frolicked in the surf, made giddy by

the late hour and pent up sexual desire, and then he swooped her up in his arms, settling her snuggly against his wide chest. His skin was cool to the touch, but together they generated that glorious heat she'd felt all evening.

"This got me into trouble once before." He jiggled her in his arms and laughed. "I didn't know a girl could punch like that."

"Woman," she corrected primly.

"Don't I know it?"

"And you were heading the other way at the time," she pointed out. "You planned to dump me in the water."

"True. But you were already wet."

She shrugged. "My brother would tell you I tend to punch first and ask questions later."

"Ah, passionate."

Chuckling, she gave him a playful tap on his chin, following it up with a quick kiss.

"You've got a one-track mind."

"Not usually, but when I'm with you, I find

it difficult to think about much else," he admitted.

They reached the fire and he set her down slowly, letting her wet body slip down the length of his. She stood there for a moment in the loose circle of his arms, her body pressed against his solid one. She felt more alive than she could remember feeling in a very long time. If nothing else came of her time in Mexico, at least she had that.

"Thank you."

"For what?"

Too embarrassed to tell him, she glanced toward the hamper.

"For the towel. I'm assuming you brought one for me."

"Yes." He reached inside the hamper and pulled out two, handing one to Marnie.

"You're very thoughtful," she murmured, wrapping the long sweep of terrycloth around her body.

And he could be, she realized again, very

thoughtful. It was a nice trait in a man, one that didn't always get combined with a broad chest, chiseled abs and nicely muscled limbs. She dried off as best she could and pulled the sweatshirt back on.

"What else do you have in there?"

"Sparkling water, wine, cheese and some grapes that I thought you could peel and then feed me as I recline on the blanket with my head pillowed in your lap."

"Have you ever sought counseling? That's a pretty rich fantasy life you have."

He only raised his brows in speculation. "We'll see."

He withdrew the bottle of wine from the hamper, along with two glass goblets whose thin stems were threaded through his fingers. Had it just been the night before that they'd shared wine from those glasses on his small patio after the sun had set?

"Would you like some wine?" he asked.

"It's a nice merlot I picked up at a winery in California."

He didn't mention that he'd bought five cases of the vintage or that the price would have put most people back by a few months worth of wages.

She divided a glance between the man and the wine.

"Sparkling water, please. I think I need to keep a clear head tonight."

"You can trust me," he said sounding so sincere that she didn't doubt that she could.

And so she admitted, "But I'm not sure I can trust myself."

To lighten the mood her confession created, she added, "You know, I didn't like you when we met."

"That came through loud and clear."

"I thought you were a jerk."

"And I thought you were a pain in the…butt." He poured water into both goblets and handed one to her. "Beautiful, of course, but a pain in the butt."

The compliment warmed Marnie more than it should have given the qualifier he'd added.

"And I thought you were handsome. Dumb as a post, but handsome."

"Dumb?"

"As a post. Yes." She sipped from her water. "I'm generalizing here, but in my experience men as good-looking as you are rarely smart, and regardless, they tend to be jerks."

"In your experience?"

"Yes."

"And would that experience be vast?"

She tipped her head to one side. "Proving my point already, are you?"

"Strike that question. What do you think of me now?"

"Hmm." She sipped the water again and mulled her answer. "Well, I think you're smart." When he smiled smugly, she added,

"Of course, the jury's still out on the jerk part."

"Did you hear that?"

She glanced around the beach. "No. What?"

"It was the sound of my ego shattering into unsalvageable bits."

"And the universe just got a bit roomier as a result," she said, clanking her glass against his. Then she grinned. "Your turn. What do *you* think of *me* now?"

In the fire's glow, J.T. studied her face. "I've never met anyone quite like you."

And the tone of his voice was as serious as his gaze was steady.

"What about me is different from other women?" The words were barely above a whisper.

"Everything," he replied just as quietly.

His gaze strayed to the fire and stayed there for the next several minutes. The silence stretched, but Marnie wasn't sure how to break it. With one simple word, something fundamental between them seemed to have shifted and fallen into place like the tumblers on a safe's lock.

Then, even though a good five minutes had passed, J.T. spoke again, picking up where he left off.

"The thing that really sets you apart is that you say what you mean. A lot of the women I've known—a lot of men, too—haven't. I like that about you. You speak your mind, no punches pulled."

She snorted out a laugh. "A little too often, to hear my family tell it."

"It's a good trait, believe me. Not a lot of people do, especially to me."

She wanted to ask what he meant, but he reached for her and at his touch, she was lost.

Their goblets were set aside hastily, and Marnie was pretty sure her water had spilled into the sand. But before things could get out of hand again, she extricated herself from his arms.

"Who knew I had this much willpower?" she said on a shaky laugh as she rose to her feet.

"I was thinking the same thing just before that swim. It's rare for me to find something—someone—so difficult to resist."

The way he was looking up at her had Marnie wanting to drop to her knees. Instead, she pulled her jangling hormones together and stepped clear of the blanket.

"I think we'd better call it a night. It's got to be after three and I have a long drive in the morning."

He nodded and stood as well. When she reached down for the blanket, intending to help him shake it out and fold it, he stopped her.

"Leave it. I think I'll stay out here for a while after you go in. I'm in no mood for going to bed just yet. At least not alone."

The walk across the beach to her door was short, but torturous. They stood on the threshold as they had not long before, but there was no teasing banter this time, no desperate groping.

"One last kiss good-night," he said.

But Marnie shook her head. She wound her arms around his neck and pulled him to her, tight against the heart that was already beginning to ache.

"Better make it goodbye, J.T."

Half an hour after the sun rose the following morning, Marnie packed up the car and took her leave. She hadn't slept at all unless one counted the fitful half-hour doze she'd fallen into just before sunup. But she didn't want to take the chance of running into J.T. on the beach. Their goodbye the night before had been too perfect to repeat. Anything they said to one another now would only be anticlimactic.

Still, she'd glanced across the sand to where they'd sat by the fire the night before. Thin spirals of smoke still curled from the charred logs, but the blanket and hamper were gone and so was J.T.

"Adios," she whispered, climbing into the car.

As she pulled the vehicle onto the road, she put "Midnight Train to Georgia" into the CD player, singing the "leaving" part along with the Pips rather than Gladys Knight. She blinked rapidly, blaming the tears that blurred her vision on the brightening skyline.

J.T. stood at the window in his kitchen and watched her go. He had an extra cup of coffee in one hand, which he now poured down the sink—a perfectly good waste of Starbucks. But then, it didn't really matter. Marnie was gone.

She'd left earlier than he'd expected she would, which was why he was up. In fact, he'd never slept. He'd sat on the beach, foolishly hoping she would change her mind and return.

The fire hadn't seemed half as cheerful without her, and the heat it generated was nothing compared to the heat burning inside him. He'd waited until nearly sunup before going inside. Then he'd ground beans and planned to surprise her with coffee. Maybe he could talk her into having breakfast with him, a morning walk to pick up those shells she found so pretty.

And then what?

The question had haunted him while he watched the coffee drip into the glass carafe, its robust aroma filling the kitchen. For the first time in years, he didn't have an answer to a problem.

Even with Terri, once confronted with her infidelity, he'd formulated a plan. Data in, decision made, plan executed. Oh, it hadn't been as tidy as that, but the course of action had been obvious, his conclusions easily reached once all of the facts were spread out before him.

But Marnie confounded him. Nothing about her was easy to compute. Funny, sexy, blunt and in control one minute, then vulnerable and almost shy the next. He hadn't been feeding her a line the night before when he'd told her he'd never met anyone like her. In one long weekend she'd managed to create more chaos in his well-ordered life than the Justice Department's investigation.

It was just as well, he supposed, that she was leaving. She'd been a nice diversion, but she was, well, too diverting, not to mention awfully adept at getting him to lower his guard.

"Adios," he called as her car sped away.

CHAPTER SEVEN

MARNIE was nearly to the U.S. border, feeling miserable and more than a little sorry for herself, although why exactly, she couldn't have said. It's not as if her long weekend could have ended any other way.

But what if…?

The question whispered in her head as the miles passed. It seemed her old nemesis had risen again. How many times had she asked that particular question since Hal's death? This time, however, the question was different. It started the same, but she couldn't quite finish it. What if…what?

Restless, that's what she felt. And she hadn't

felt that way in years. The sensation was as liberating as it was revealing.

The road sign pointed the direction to the United States border. Marnie turned off, following the exit to Tijuana. Maybe she'd just do a little more sightseeing and souvenir gathering before heading back. Shopping had always proved to be a good way to clear her mind.

In the second store she browsed through, she spotted a gorgeous printed scarf. The fabric was so soft it felt like silk, but the price tag told her differently. Still, she bought it—bought three, in fact, in a variety of colors and designs. They all went well with the skirt she picked up dirt cheap in a neighboring shop. It wasn't as well made as she would have liked, but she'd seen something similar in a fashion magazine last month while waiting in the dentist office. The style, she knew, would flatter her. In fact, it would flatter most women, regardless of their body type.

She paid for her purchases and, instead of heading back to the car, found a little outdoor café where she ordered bottled water and a spicy rice and beans concoction that made her appreciate the beverage.

After her plate and utensils had been cleared away, she sat there for a moment, sipping the last of the water and enjoying the sunshine. It would be cold in Michigan's U.P., barely above freezing in the evenings if it had warmed up that much. It would be a while yet before she could wear any of the things she had purchased in Yuma or on her excursion today.

She pulled the scarves from the bag and ran her hand over the fabric again. The women in Chance Harbor were going to be so envious, she thought with an absent smile. No area stores carried anything quite like these. In fact, those stores didn't carry much to appeal to any woman who wanted to set trends or follow fashion.

She rubbed the fabric again and, as if it were the side of a genie's lamp, the dream of owning her own mail-order fashion business floated before her.

Was it still possible? Could she *make* it possible?

Once upon a time, she'd believed that hard work and sheer determination were all it took to accomplish anything. She hadn't placed much stock in luck, but now she knew that some things, some circumstances were beyond her control. Good luck, bad luck—both played a role.

And yet lately she'd begun to think maybe it was time to apply her will so she could make her way. Lately she'd begun to think that maybe her future didn't have to be dictated by the past or even the present.

Metaphorically speaking, she'd been trudging along dutifully in her well-worn rut since Hal's death. Mason called it a holding pattern and, loving pain in the butt that her brother was, he'd done his best to goad her out of it on more than one occasion. All of her friends and family had. But she'd failed to rise to the bait. She simply hadn't been ready.

Was she ready now?

Marnie wanted to be. She wasn't one to wallow in self-pity and the inertia it often created. She wanted to do something more than exist. She'd been trying to work her way back to the land of the living for quite some time now, but this chance trip to Mexico—and a few hours of stolen passion with a virtual stranger— seemed to have helped her start the journey.

She wouldn't, couldn't think about the passion part now. But the business part, well that was another story. So, she set aside the scarves and rummaged through her purse for a pen and a small pad of paper. For the next hour she made notes, cracking open the door, at least in her mind, to the long-closed Marnie's Closet.

When she finished, she realized there was

much more she needed to consider. It would take longer than a single afternoon to put all of these ducks in a row, to wrap her mind around the many possibilities and pitfalls that loomed ahead of her. Clearly, she needed more time to ruminate, and she needed peace and quiet, the kind the working mother of a preschooler rarely got to enjoy.

She knew the perfect place.

She paid her bill, went in search of a pay phone and placed a couple of calls, one to her parents and one to the tavern in Chance Harbor. She was humming "Ain't No Mountain High Enough" when she got into the car and gunned its engine to life. By the time she was back on the highway she was belting out the lyrics as well.

South. That's what the highway sign said, but she knew that more than her direction had changed.

All the way back to La Playa de la Pisada, Marnie told herself J.T.'s presence on that small sweep of beach had done nothing to sway her decision to return. It was the peace and quiet she needed to really think this plan through. That's what she craved at this point. Not his touch. Certainly not his kiss.

Then she pulled up next to the old shack she'd rented once again and saw him rising up out of the water sans swim trunks. He looked like some mythical glistening god and his lack of a tan line told her this was his preferred method of sunbathing. Marnie admitted there was indeed a side benefit to choosing this particular location for her sojourn.

He didn't see her, at least not at first. He dried off before wrapping the towel around his hips. And Marnie couldn't help herself, she blasted the horn. He jumped—nearly out of his skin, and nicely out of his towel for a second or two before he managed to secure it into place again and walk to where she stood leaning again the car door.

"You're back." His expression was unreadable.

"Yes."

Then one side of his mouth crooked up. "Did you forget something?"

Her gaze slid down his chest before she snapped it back to his face. No, she hadn't forgotten a thing. It was all *exactly* as she remembered it, burned onto her corneas, as a matter of fact.

"I've decided to extend my stay."

"You don't say?" His smile was slow and potent. "What made you change your mind?"

"Oh, this, that—" her gaze dipped fractionally despite her best efforts "—and the other."

"How long will you be here?"

"A couple more weeks. I have some things to sort out and thought this might be a good place to do it. The view is rather inspiring."

"More so now," he agreed. "I planned to leave in a few days."

"Oh."

It hadn't dawned on her that he might have to return to wherever it was that he came from.

"That was the plan anyway," he added.

"And will you now?"

"Depends."

"On what?"

He hesitated only a moment before asking, "Do you want me to stay?"

Marnie blew out a long breath. She wasn't sure what she wanted when it came to this confounding man. No, that wasn't true. She wanted J.T. physically. She was adult enough to admit it. But she was also responsible enough not to act on mere impulse, consequences be damned.

The if-it-feels-good philosophy had never been one she'd lived by. So the fact that she wanted him didn't change the fact that she barely knew him and they might not see one another again after this brief interlude.

And, of course, there was the matter of his profession. She couldn't see herself getting tangled up with someone who chased bail-jumpers and other potentially dangerous degenerates for a living. She had Noah to think about. Her son's needs would always trump her own.

"If I say yes, it doesn't mean I plan to sleep with you."

A smile lurked in J.T.'s gaze and he stepped forward, trapping her between his cool wet skin and the hard heated steel of the car. Both were unyielding, but only one made her want to lean in and sigh.

"Fair enough. But do I get to try to talk you into it?"

"Well, if you must."

No harm in that, she decided, as he leaned down, nipped her lower lip.

"I must," he said, before kissing her in earnest.

They prepared dinner in J.T.'s kitchen, falling into an easy camaraderie that Marnie found almost as alluring as the sexual sparks they struck off one another. J.T. generously offered to cook their meal after she related the story of how she'd once burned pork chops so badly that Chance Harbor's volunteer fire department had to be called to her home.

"Do you still live in this house? Or was it burned beyond rehabilitation?" he teased.

"No. It's still standing."

"From what I know of you, I'm guessing you live in a sprawling ranch, maybe with a built-in pool tucked into the yard. And all of it is surrounded by a tall privacy fence, of course, so that you could sunbathe in the nude should the mood strike."

"That's a disturbingly detailed fantasy," she replied as she sat at the table, tearing up greens for a salad. "But highly impractical. In northern Michigan an outdoor pool of any sort would be a labor of love. In my opinion, the season's too short to make it worth all of the work. But my house does have a nice little yard and a great view of Superior."

"No nude sunbathing?"

"Sorry. And before you ask, I won't be doing any of that while I'm here, either."

He groaned. "Was I at least right about the ranch part?"

"Nope. Actually, it's a bungalow. Not big, but big enough. Three bedrooms, one bath. It's an older home, not many new-builds in Chance Harbor, but we remodeled it, added a fancy tub with jets."

"We?"

She stopped, stared at the shredded lettuce in her hands. Memories beckoned, bitter-sweet, but no longer quite so painful. "My husband and I," she said softly.

"I seem to recall you telling me once that you weren't married."

He had gone still as well and his tone had chilled by several degrees. Marnie barely no-ticed, caught up as she was in the past.

"I'm not. Now. Hal…died." Saying the word no longer made her ache or want to cry. When had that happened? she wondered.

"I'm sorry, Marnie."

"It was three years ago." J.T. hadn't asked how, but she supplied the information anyway. "It was an accident. He went through the ice trying to save some snowmobilers. And he did. Save them, I mean."

"I'm sure you miss him."

Miss him? Oh, yes, she did. He was her first love and Noah's father. For those two reasons alone, she would love Hal forever. But something had changed, something fundamental. Thinking back, she realized that it had begun, appropriately enough for her, in a dressing room in a Yuma department store and had continued after she arrived in Mexico. Suddenly she knew what it was.

"Hal was a good man, but I've learned that life has a way of moving forward, even when we try to stay put."

He walked to where she sat at his table and placed one big hand on her shoulder. The pressure was comforting, as were his words when he told her, "It takes strength and courage to move forward."

Marnie wiped her hands on a towel and then placed one over his, giving it a squeeze. It also took courage to dream, she realized, and that's exactly what she was doing. Then she glanced up at J.T., returned his warm smile and a question niggled: Was starting a new business her *only* dream?

"I can make the rice," she offered hastily.

She felt pretty confident she could manage that since it came with a little packet of seasonings and the directions were printed clearly on the side of the box.

"Let me get out the fire extinguisher first." The remark earned J.T. a black look.

Wisely he slipped out the door to put a couple of steaks he'd marinated on the grill before she could respond.

When the meat and rice were done, they sat down at the table in his kitchen. The sun was setting and the room seemed gloomy until Marnie lit the scented candle J.T. kept on the stove to chase away cooking odors. She set it in the center of the table, surrounding it with the shells she'd collected on the beach earlier in the day.

J.T. smiled as he watched her. It was such a fussy, female thing and yet he'd always appreciated those touches. Indeed, they were one of the few things he actually missed about being married to Terri.

"Care for some wine?" he asked.

"Maybe just a little."

He opted for Chianti instead of merlot and chose Sarah Vaughn's bluesy tunes instead of classic Motown. The setting was intimate but homey, and it made J.T. realize how much he'd missed simple dinners with a woman, with a family. He recalled sitting around the table with his sister and parents when he was a kid. He and Anne would bicker over music while his folks discussed their work days or debated politics.

Nothing had been that pure or simple since he'd made his first million. For all his money, J.T. knew there were some things it couldn't buy. Happiness was the obvious, if cliché, one. But companionship, *real* companionship, rated right up there, too.

Perhaps he'd spent too much time in the sun, but something seemed to be happening here: Something solid or at least the beginning of something that could grow into much more with care, nurturing and a little old-fashioned hard work. Of course, he'd have to level with Marnie, throw off the mantle of secrecy before anything could develop fully. Was he prepared to do that?

"Why don't you open the wine? It needs to breathe," he said.

And so do I, J.T. thought, as he stood and

walked to the stove on the pretext of retrieving the pepper mill.

What if he was wrong? They'd known each other mere days, after all. He and Terri had dated a couple of years before tying the knot and he'd still been far off the mark when it came to gauging her true feelings.

He would keep quiet for now, he decided. He'd never been one to rush into things and, besides, nothing might come of this affair, if it could be called that when Marnie had made it clear she didn't plan to sleep with him.

He returned to the table, intending to keep the conversation light, but the words that slipped out were: "What are we doing?"

"Having dinner."

"That's not what I meant."

She had picked up her fork. Now she set it aside. "I know. I'm not sure. Do we have to know?"

When he opened his mouth to speak, she held up one hand. "Let me finish, please. I've spent the past three years never straying from the beaten path, believing I couldn't stray because I have a s-...I have responsibilities. For the first time in a long time, I'm not interested in following that well-worn road before me. I came to Mexico to get away from people who think of me as Poor Marnie LaRue, and I decided to stay in Mexico to make plans for my future. New plans. Bigger plans. You have to have dreams," she said, and he swore she was trying to convince herself as well as him with her impassioned speech.

"You're an unexpected..." Her voice trailed away.

"Bonus?" he supplied.

A smile bloomed on her otherwise serious face. "I was going to say complication, but that, too. Can we be friends?"

The statement made sense, but J.T. couldn't help himself, he winced.

"That's just what a guy wants to hear," he muttered, finding that he was as amused by her words as he was put out. How was it possible that Marnie managed to inspire both emotions in him at the same time? Exasperating, that's what she was. "Next you'll be telling me I'm special."

"You are."

"So, we're going to be really good friends for the next couple weeks?"

She nodded.

"And then?"

Marnie blinked slowly and said, "I guess we'll go our separate ways."

The words were no less than what he'd expected her to say, and they seemed to validate his decision to hold his tongue. Yet, J.T. found himself wanting to convince her otherwise.

He didn't sleep much that night. He'd tossed and turned, vivid dreams of a scantily clad Marnie mocking his libido. A mere hour after sunrise the next morning, he decided to walk over to her place and rouse her from sleep as well. She was the cause of his insomnia, so it was only fair that she pay. He wasn't a complete ogre, though. He did bring coffee—an entire insulated carafe full of Starbucks' Breakfast Blend.

But when he arrived at Marnie's door and raised his hand to knock, he spied her through the window. She was up already and seated at the table, the burned down nub of a fat candle acting as a centerpiece. She wore a lacey tank top over a stingy pair of shorts. The pale, soft fabric told him the outfit served as pajamas. But it wasn't the way she filled them out that gave him pause. It was the fact that from the neck up, she looked all business as she sat furiously writing down something, bottom lip caught in her teeth, and a pair of small, dark rectangular glasses balanced on her nose.

Wheels were turning, gears shifting in that pretty head of hers. He could almost hear them. His stomach clenched, familiar suspicions lurching forward. What was she up to?

He knocked, determined to find out.

Marnie glanced up at the sound, caught sight of him in the window and motioned for him to come inside.

"I'm surprised to find you up," he said.

"Couldn't sleep." She pulled off the glasses and set them aside. "I've been up for hours."

"Thinking of me?" he asked, trying to keep his tone light.

She regarded him with an absent smile. "Business, actually."

He frowned. Business? She'd told him she tended bar at her family's tavern. Surely that didn't require a predawn planning session while on vacation several thousand miles away.

"Is something wrong?" she asked.

He wanted to confront her, but he shook his head instead, biding his time.

He held out the carafe of coffee. "If you've got a couple of cups, I brought something to fill them with."

The promise of caffeine had Marnie grinning. In short order, she hunted up two mugs and rejoined him at the table.

"So, what is this business that has you up and out of bed at such an ungodly hour?" he asked nonchalantly.

Over the rim of his mug, J.T. tried to decipher her handwriting, but the woman's penmanship left something to be desired, especially since he was trying to read it upside down.

She gathered up the notes and turned the pages over, resting her mug on top of them as if it were a paperweight.

"It's just an idea I've been kicking around."

Was it his imagination, or did she seem evasive all of a sudden?

"Mind if I take a look?"

"Yes!" Her tone was sharp, but then she smiled as if to lessen the sting. "I mean, it's just some notes. They won't make any sense to you. They barely make sense to me. This may very well wind up being a pipedream."

"Ah."

"This coffee tastes great, by the way."

She lifted her mug for another sip, effectively changing the subject. He decided to let it drop for now.

"First cup is always the best," he agreed.

"I was planning to go out for a walk on the beach after I finished up here. Care to join me?"

"Make it a jog and you've got a deal."

"I don't care for running," she replied.

"Well, if you don't think you can keep up…?"

Her eyes narrowed in challenge. "I'll set the pace."

"Of course," he said dryly as their relationship seemed to slip back onto familiar footing.

They jogged up the beach for a little more than a mile before Marnie finally admitted she needed to rest. And J.T., bless his heart, had been gentleman enough to pretend it was for his benefit that he suggested walking on the way back.

She had another handful of seashells by the time they reached his house. She set them on the patio table and settled into one of the chairs.

"It's a gorgeous day," she said, tilting her face up for the sun's kiss.

Marnie couldn't remember the last time she'd felt this happy, this full of hope for the future. She thought about the notes she'd made, the plans she intended to put into motion as soon as she returned to Chance Harbor. She'd downplayed it as a pipedream when J.T. had asked about it that morning. It had still seemed too fragile to expose to scrutiny, but it had bumped around in her head throughout their run, seeming to grow bigger with each passing minute until finally she could no longer contain it.

"I'm going to start my own business," she blurted out, apropos of nothing. She shook her head and stole a sheepish glance at J.T. "I can't believe I just said it out loud. I've hardly whispered it to myself in three long years."

"You'd be surprised how often people tell me similar things," he replied. And although the words seemed teasing, his tone was oddly serious when he said carefully, "So, what kind of business are you thinking of starting?"

"Mail-order fashions for women."

She hadn't talked about it to anyone in so long that it surprised her that the exuberance was still there, bubbling to the surface as she spoke.

"I plan to start small, offering just women's clothes and later branch out into men's and children's fashions. Far down the line, I was thinking about home furnishings and accent pieces. I'd like it to be a little upscale, but not so far out of reach that people glance at the catalog and then toss it in the trash once they catch a glimpse of the prices."

"It takes a lot of money to start a business,"

he remarked mildly, his gaze fixed on the horizon.

"Tell me about it. That's been one of my biggest stumbling blocks."

"But it's not now?"

"Yes and no. My parents were just telling me the other day about some loan programs for women entrepreneurs, but since I've been in Mexico I realized that, if all else fails, I do have another funding source I might be able to tap for some cash."

She said the words hesitantly, unaware of J.T.'s frown.

Hal's insurance money. The sum wasn't a fortune, but it represented a nice little nest egg. She had stashed it away into a savings account, drawing interest. It was to be Noah's college fund. Was she really considering raiding it to follow her dream?

If need be—yes, she realized. If the business tanked and she lost her shirt, she would remortgage her house when Noah turned eighteen so that she could send him to whatever university he wanted to attend. In the meantime, however, it would do him good to see his mother wanting something more and working doggedly to achieve it.

You have to follow your dreams.

Hal had told her that, and it had taken Marnie awhile to realize that her late husband's dream had been far less grand than what she had wanted for him, or for the pair of them. His dream had been Marnie and Noah and the small bungalow on Superior. He hadn't wanted a more prestigious job or even a college diploma.

She accepted that now, just as she accepted that she wanted much, much more. More than she could even fully comprehend at the moment. That didn't make her greedy. It made her ambitious.

"Where would you get cash like that?" J.T. inquired, breaking into her thoughts.

She couldn't confide in him about the insurance money. It seemed too, well, selfish. So, she winked and told him instead, "I've got a sugar daddy in mind."

J.T. had watched the emotions play over Marnie's lovely face. There had been wonder and excitement brimming in those slow-blinking eyes until something that seemed suspiciously like guilt had settled in their place.

Sugar daddy? She'd said it jokingly, but it nonetheless made him wonder: Did she think he might be that unplumbed resource to which she had previously referred?

The possibility disappointed J.T. deeply, even though he'd lost count of the number of times people—friends, family, strangers even—had approached him about backing some business proposition or another. The interest-free loans he'd made to people over the years didn't bother him much, even though only a handful had ever been repaid. He could afford to throw money at their endeavors, dubious or otherwise. But that didn't mean he didn't sometimes resent like hell being the Bank of J.T.

He waited, held his breath actually, expecting Marnie to ask for a loan. Had she had finally put it all together? He had told her his last name that evening in Ensenada.

J.T. Lundy. It wasn't particularly difficult to extrapolate out from that to Jonathon Thomas Lundy, president and founder of Tracker Operating Systems and one of the world's wealthiest businessmen.

Or, if she hadn't figured out his actual identity, maybe she just assumed that based on the quality furnishings in his vacation home, he could afford to pony up a tidy little sum for her venture.

But the only question she asked was, "What are you making for breakfast?"

"Breakfast?"

"I'm thinking eggs, sausage, the works. I'm famished after all of that exercise."

"Kitchen's right in there," he said, pointing

over his shoulder and feeling ridiculously relieved that the only thing she was seeking at the moment was food.

She smiled, letting loose the full wattage of her considerable charm. "But you are the better cook."

And J.T., whose signature appeared on the paychecks of tens of thousands of workers and who had hired help at his Silicon Valley mansion to see to his every need, found himself getting up to do Marnie LaRue's bidding.

CHAPTER EIGHT

"YOU'RE a regular Julia Child in the kitchen, J.T.," Marnie said as she pushed away from the table and settled back in her chair, stuffed and content.

It was nice having someone wait on her for a change, but that wasn't the only reason for her satisfied smile. She'd also gotten out of doing the dishes. Again. He'd cleared the table and was up to his elbows in soapy water even before she'd drained the last of her coffee. Even with a striped dish towel draped negligently over one shoulder and performing what many a chauvinist still considered "woman's work," he looked downright masculine and unaccountably sexy.

"Thanks," he muttered, but he was smiling.

Before their meal, he'd seemed distracted, on edge even. But now he appeared relaxed once more. Maybe she had just imagined that for a while there he'd seemed so distant.

"So, where did you learn to cook?"

"My mother. She taught both my sister and me the basics." He chuckled then. "Said she didn't want me to starve to death after I moved out of the house."

"Let me guess. You lived on pizza instead?"

"Have you been talking to my mother?"

"No, I have a brother, remember. He lived on fast food and frozen dinners until he decided to put his limited culinary skills to work. My mom insisted we both learn the basics as well."

"What happened to you?"

She sent him a black look. "I can boil water and operate a microwave."

"Talented."

"I'm going to be the bigger person and ignore your sarcasm," she sniffed. "So, do you see your parents often?"

"Not so much now. Work keeps me pretty busy."

"Not to mention on the road. Your job must take you all over the place."

"Yeah." J.T. coughed and when he spoke again, he'd changed the subject. "You know, this day's too nice to spend indoors. Sometimes in April it can still be chilly and rainy down here."

She glanced out the window. No rain on the horizon this day. The sun was shining in a cloudless blue sky, so it was warm despite a stiff breeze that churned in off the ocean.

"What do you want to do today?" she asked.

He pulled the dish towel off his shoulder and wiped his hands. "I was thinking about taking another road trip, if you're up for one that is?"

"I might be so inclined." She grinned. "Do you have a destination in mind?"

"I was thinking about heading south this time. To El Rosario and then maybe inland to Catavina. It's rugged and dry there. Lots of cacti and rock formations and even some cave paintings. I thought you might like to bring along your camera and take some pictures."

"Sounds like a full day."

He consulted his watch and then rubbed his chin, as if considering. "Better pack an overnight bag."

"An overnight bag?" Marnie asked, narrowing her eyes in suspicion.

"It's already almost ten o'clock. By the time we get around—I'm assuming you'll need to shower?"

"God, yes!"

"Well, half the day will be gone before we get on the road and then there's travel time. It's a couple hours, give or take, to El Rosario and then another hour or so in to Catavina, assuming we make no other stops." He shrugged innocently. "It just makes sense to be prepared."

Her tone was still doubtful when she said, "So, you're not hoping to have your way with me on the lumpy mattress in some hotel room?"

Innocence was gone in a flash, the smile on his handsome face replaced by one so bold and lethal that it caused her breath to hitch and her heart to quake. Lord, would she ever get used to the way one smoldering look from him could yank the proverbial rug out from beneath her feet?

"Of course, that's what I'm hoping, Marnie. God help me, but I want you."

Their gazes locked across the small kitchen and even with a dishtowel still clutched in one hand, he looked dangerous and, for some reason, angry.

"Well…well…" she stammered, but could think of nothing to say in reply to so blunt a statement. Marnie was a firm believer in speaking her mind, but it had gone alarmingly blank.

"I'm just giving you fair warning. I know where you stand on the subject of our sleeping together. I'm just making sure you know where I stand. I want you," he said again. "I didn't plan to feel this way. In fact, I'm not sure I like feeling this way. But there it is—a reality that can't be ignored."

"We hardly know one another," she whispered. The reminder was as much for her own benefit as it was for his, she realized, when she felt that tempting tug of attraction begin to pull at her once again.

He acknowledged her point with a curt nod of his head.

"I plan to change that. Starting today. So, what do you say? Are you still up for that road trip?"

She hesitated a moment, mulling over J.T.'s words.

I want you.

The bald statement hardly came as a surprise given what had already transpired between them. And he'd said as much before, but that was in the heat of passion, not while they were companionably conversing over the breakfast table. Oddly, this setting gave his words more impact, more urgency, even a greater sense of intimacy.

"If I say yes, it doesn't mean yes to *everything*," she stressed.

"So noted."

They passed the time spent driving to El Rosario in surprisingly easy conversation. J.T. wasn't sure what had possessed him to offer to get better acquainted, but he made good on it. What he told Marnie might not have been the whole, unvarnished truth, but it was far more than the sterile tidbits contained in his official biography.

"My sister, Anne, is a photographer. She lives just outside San Francisco, not far from me as a matter of fact. She had her first gallery show back in December," he said, "It went really well."

"You live in California?"

"Yes." And then he held his breath after adding, "Near Silicon Valley."

"Oh, my God!"

J.T. braced himself for the revelation, but he needn't have bothered. Marnie's response was not what he expected. It wasn't even in the ballpark.

"That's her work on the walls in your living room in La Playa de la Pisada, isn't it?"

"Anne's, yes." And he relaxed enough to smile. "She's good, huh?"

"Very. And I have to admit, I'm relieved to discover the photographer is your sister."

"Why?"

"I figured whoever had taken those pictures, especially the one of you gazing down a mountainside while standing on some ski slope, knew you well. She captured you at such an unguarded moment. I assumed it was a lover," Marnie admitted.

He flicked a surprised look her way and

watched her face heat to crimson. Had she been jealous? And, if so, why did that make him feel so ridiculously pleased?

"Are the two of you close?" she asked hastily.

"Yes. My folks adopted Anne when she was still in diapers. I didn't like her much when she first arrived," he admitted with a rueful chuckle. "Didn't really care for the idea of sharing my parents' attention, I guess. But I was eight and she was two—small for her age and so serious all of the time. It didn't take long before I'd tumbled under her spell same as my folks. Then, even when I was complaining that she was getting into my stuff, I kind of got a kick out of being her big brother."

Marnie grinned, letting her own childhood memories come. They played through her mind like the reel of a Disney movie. Time had smoothed out the rougher edges—squabbles with Mason and her mother and the usual teenage angst and pimple crises—until only happy images remained. She was lucky, she thought. Not many people had that. But it appeared J.T. had. It appeared he enjoyed a strong bond with his sister even now that they had gone their separate ways in life. Marnie liked that about him, since she and her brother had that kind of relationship.

"I'm close with my brother," she said. "He's older than me as well—five years. And we fought plenty as kids. But I know I can count on him. If I called him right now and told him I needed him, he'd catch the next plane out, no questions asked."

"Anne, too," J.T. said thoughtfully.

"What about your folks? Are they in California?" she asked.

"Yes. They retired a few years back and moved not far from Anne and me. They're eager for grandbabies, but Anne's not married yet." He chuckled softly. "They keep trying to set her up with their neighbors' sons."

"What about you? Do they try to set you up?"

"Nah. They've given up on me," he said with a laugh.

Of course, J.T. knew that wasn't true. Just a month earlier, his mother had called to tell him about a nice young woman who worked in the office of the podiatrist she saw.

"I've got her number," his mother had told him. But J.T. had refused to take it.

Blind dates had rarely proved to be anything but disappointing in his experience, and that had been long before he'd been christened the World's Sexiest CEO by *Faces* magazine or joined the exclusive ranks of billionaires.

"So, did you grow up in California?" Marnie asked.

"Nope. Iowa."

She stared at him, mouth dropping open for a moment before she sputtered, "You're a former farm boy?"

"Des Moines," he clarified. "There are more than cornfields in the state, you know."

"What made you move to California?"

"College. I got a scholarship to UCLA."

"Hmm. Let me guess." She reached across the Jeep's console to give his bicep a friendly squeeze. "Football scholarship?"

"Actually, academic."

"Really?"

She must have realized that her one-word response could be taken as an insult, because she amended it nicely with, "I-I'm just surprised since you look like you would have played football. I mean you're what, six-two?"

"Six-three."

"Uh-huh."

He watched her swallow.

"And you're…muscular."

"Thank you."

It might have been a trick of the light, but he thought she was blushing again.

"Were you on the team in high school?"

He nearly laughed out loud and might have if such a reaction wouldn't have required an explanation. High school was still a not-so-pleasant memory for him. His interest in and knowledge of computers and operating systems made him a force to be reckoned with now, but back then such pursuits had been a liability when it came to social acceptance. Add to that the fact that he'd passed the six-foot mark at fourteen, but without adding much heft to his build, and he'd been a walking definition of the word geek. No matter how much he'd eaten, he hadn't gained an ounce—not until just after college when the pounds finally started to stick to his frame. Now he was thankful for his fast metabolism, which allowed him to overindulge on occasion without spending more time with the personal trainer in his home gym. Back then, of course, he had cursed it.

"I wasn't much into sports as a kid."

"What were you into?"

"Computers."

"A computer nerd? You?" Marnie laughed outright. "That's hard for me to picture."

"True nonetheless, I'm afraid."

"Why computers?" she asked, sounding truly intrigued.

He shrugged. Why breathe? might be as good a question. He'd been hooked after the first time he'd sat down in front of a keyboard in a computer programming class as a teenager. He'd idolized Steve Jobs—co-founder of the Apple Computer Corporation—the way most kids idolized basketball players or Hollywood action heroes. And he'd wanted to be just like Jobs—a multimillionaire before he hit thirty. He'd gotten his wish as the chief architect of some of the most efficient and innovative software on the market.

"They've always fascinated me. All that power and potential just keystrokes away."

"I find technology alternately baffling and terrifying," she admitted on a sigh.

"Have you ever thought about taking a class? Once you understand the basics, it's not so intimidating."

"Oh, I've taken a class—just last winter as a matter of fact. The public school system offered a community education course. I understand the basics and I've even used what I learned to help keep track of inventory and expenses at the tavern. But beyond the basics, it's all Greek to me."

She squinted sideways at him. "If you tell me you speak that language, I'll have to hurt you."

"Not yet. But getting back to computers, they're worth the hassle of figuring out how to use them, especially if you're serious about this business idea you mentioned."

Her face lit up then. Determination, ambition. J.T. had seen both emotions enough times to recognize them. And yet he'd never thought of them as sexy until just now.

"Oh, I'm serious. I've already made some

notes about the kind of website I'd like to have designed. I figure my bottom line will rely heavily on Internet traffic, since more and more people do their shopping on-line these days."

"Smart thinking," he said.

"Well, technology has changed the way people do business."

He nodded in agreement. "It's changed our lifestyles, too. Telecommuting, instant messaging, on-line banking. Rather than consulting a map we click on MapQuest."

"Men, maybe. Women still have no problem asking for directions."

He rolled his eyes and continued. "My point is that advanced technology has made our lives more convenient and our time easier to manage."

"Yes, where would we be without our Palm Pilots, cell phones and the capability to illegally download the latest movies and music?" she asked drolly.

But he wasn't deterred. "Admit it. Just like the invention of the telephone and the airplane, computers have made the planet a smaller place. People on opposite ends of the Earth can converse through e-mail. Computers and the Internet help keep people connected. They help make the differences that divide us that much more inconsequential when compared to what we have in common."

"But some people would say computers have separated us, too. Instead of going out to socialize, we sit alone in our homes and have conversations with people we may never meet in person. People who can lie and say they are wealthy or important or attractive or single when in fact they might be none of those things."

"Virtual reality," he murmured. "Who's to say what's real anyway?"

"I value truth," Marnie replied and he inwardly winced. "And reality is not whatever someone deems it to be for convenience's sake. People can't change who they are."

"No, but they can pretend for a little while. Is there harm in that?"

"Sometimes, yes."

"Why?"

"Read a newspaper. What about stalkers and other assorted perverts who prey on teenage girls pretending to be something they aren't?"

"Touché." And he decided to let that line of thinking go, realizing he only had been looking for a way to rationalize withholding the truth from her.

But he couldn't let the topic drop before adding, "I still say computers are among the greatest inventions of the twentieth century. Consider what the world would be like today without the Internet or software that is cost-effective and efficient to use."

Such passion, Marnie thought, as she listened to him expound on the subject for the next several minutes. And despite the fact that she didn't know a gigabyte from a go-cart it was clear that he did.

They were nearly to El Rosario when she said, "If the bounty hunter thing doesn't work out, you should consider a career as a computer programmer or something."

His gaze cut her way and he opened his mouth to say something, but then he only smiled.

J.T. wanted to confide in Marnie about his identity and put to rest the specter of him being a bounty hunter, fascinating and flattering as he found that fabrication to be. What white-collared desk jockey, after all, would mind being mistaken for the rough-and-tumble sort who chased down outlaws and hunted wanted men for a living? Titles like president, CEO or chief software architect paled in comparison, especially when paychecks were left out of the equation.

The words were there on the tip of his tongue, but then he thought about the sugar daddy comment she'd made earlier. The old adage "once burned, twice shy" proved too true. He couldn't make himself tell her.

Perhaps he was being selfish and unfair, but he needed to know exactly where he stood with Marnie as J.T. the man before he introduced the subject of his bank account. Who knew where this was leading anyway? Yes, he wanted her, but their relationship might never move beyond a mere holiday flirtation or fling. And so he decided to keep mum for now, on that subject at least.

"What about you? What were you like in high school?" His gaze drifted over her figure. "I'm guessing you were a cheerleader."

"Guilty."

"And homecoming queen."

"Guilty as well. I was also voted nicest smile," she said with a dazzling grin. Then she sobered. "But, really, I wasn't a complete vacuum. I was no member of Mensa, but I did graduate with honors. What about you?"

He'd been valedictorian and voted most likely to succeed. And he knew he had, just as he knew that his success had come at a steep personal price. And so he steered the conversation to what he considered a safer subject.

"I did participate in the debate team my senior year."

He waited for more laughter or good-natured ribbing. Instead she said quietly, "Did your school have a chess club by any chance?"

"Yep. You're looking at the captain of the state championship team three years running."

"Oh, God," she moaned.

"What?" He started to pull the Jeep to the side of the road. She looked so pale suddenly. "Are you okay?"

"I'm fine. Please, keep driving. I just…it must have been something I ate. It's passing, really."

But it wasn't passing. Marnie felt her already compromised footing begin to slip further where J.T. was concerned. It's not fair, she thought. She hadn't seen this complication coming at all. But there was no denying it. J.T. Lundy was the whole package: Smart, sexy, funny, drop-dead gorgeous.

And dangerous.

Not just because of what he did for a living, although that was bad enough, but because of what he was already doing to her heart.

CHAPTER NINE

THEY spent the majority of the day just outside Catavina, hiking over the rocky terrain and taking in the scenery. The area was beautiful in a stark way that reminded Marnie somewhat of Michigan's rugged, glacier-hewn Upper Peninsula. Sparse and untamed, both places enjoyed an understated beauty. Unlike the U.P., though, cacti grew here and mountains rose up high in the distance, far greater than the Porcupines, providing a majestic backdrop.

She used up the film on one disposable camera and fished a second one from the small backpack that doubled as a purse. This one was a Gucci knockoff that she'd picked up on a weekend trip to Chicago with Hal right after they were married. Those were happy times, she mused, running her fingers over the bag's supple brown leather.

Her gaze drifted to J.T., who stood beside her. He was waiting as patiently as a hired guide, squinting into the sun as a lazy smile lifted the corners of his mouth—a mouth that had kissed her breathless mere minutes earlier.

And Marnie knew—*these* were good times, too.

J.T. turned then and she smiled at him.

"Let me take your picture in front of those rocks, with that big cactus just behind you."

He seemed to hesitate a moment, but finally he moved to where she'd pointed. And then with the click of a button on a six-dollar disposable camera, she had immortalized him on film. Photograph or no photograph, she knew little about this man would escape her memory. More than his powerful build and chiseled features had left an impression on her. His intelligence and self-deprecating sense of humor, which she still found surprising, had as well. A lot was brewing beneath that seemingly placid surface of his. It made her want to dive right in, even as it also made her eager to keep her distance emotionally.

Why was it that this man could bring out such contradictory emotions in her?

"Want to take a break?" he asked.

"Yes…no!"

His brows tugged together. "Well, which is it? Are you tired or not?"

"Oh, from hiking."

And she wanted to slap herself for saying that aloud and making herself sound like such an idiot.

"What else would we take a break from?"

"Hiking, obviously," Marnie said airily and settled herself on a large rock.

They had hiked a ways off the beaten path, but J.T. had come prepared with bottled water and some peanuts, almonds, sunflower seeds and raisins that he had the audacity to call trail mix.

"Where's the chocolate?" Marnie asked, inspecting the handful she'd taken from the brown paper bag he'd held out to her.

"There's no chocolate in trail mix."

"Sure there is. M&M's, chocolate-covered peanuts or whatever." She slanted a look at him. "I think there might even be a law that says sugar must be supplied in equal proportion to salt in snacks such as these."

"You're nuts," he said and tossed a handful of the mix into his mouth.

"No, *these* are nuts." She held out her hand, palm open, for him to inspect. "With a few shriveled raisins thrown in."

"Well, there's something for your sweet tooth, and just for the record, all raisins are shriveled."

"These are extra-shriveled," she complained, trying to tuck away her smile. God, she enjoyed goading him. "And they're not up to the job. Unless raisins are doused in milk chocolate, they don't count. This isn't really trail mix."

"I made it and I say it is. This is a trail," he said, pointing toward the path they were tak-ing. "And this assortment of dried fruit and nuts qualifies as a mix. Put it together and you get trail mix."

"But M&M's would be nice," she muttered, not quite able to suppress a grin.

He snatched Marnie off the rock and yanked her close, kissing her so quickly that she had no time to think, only to enjoy. His lips left hers after a moment of sensual exploration to roam across her cheek, and Marnie felt his tongue tease the lobe of her ear, sucking on it lightly before he nipped at it with his teeth.

She gulped in a breath and felt her knees turn to rubber.

"Wh-what was that for?"

"Just taking your advice and balancing out the salty with something sweet." He grinned lazily then. "Although that pretty mouth of yours can be plenty tart, too. Are you always this contrary?"

"It's a gift."

"Seems more like a curse from where I'm standing."

She blinked slowly but moved fast, letting her hands glide up his chest until they reached his shoulders and drew him to her. She kissed him this time, exploring his mouth more thoroughly than they had explored the rugged Catavania countryside. She nipped his lower lip as the kiss ended, satisfied with the soft groan of pleasure he issued. No one would ever say Marnie LaRue didn't give as good as she got.

"You were saying?"

"Gift, definitely a gift," he told her.

An hour later, they both decided they needed more to sustain them than chocolate-free trail mix.

"I know a small place about an hour from

here where we can grab a bite to eat. Nothing fancy mind you, but the food is plenty filling."

"Señor Lundy, so good to see you again. And this is a new face you bring to see us. She is prettier than the last one," the café owner, Juanita Garza, teased him in Spanish.

"The last one was my sister," he reminded her.

But it did no good. She merely winked at him, "Of course. Your sister. And is this one your sister as well?"

"No, she's…a friend," he supplied in Spanish after a pause.

But he knew that with that tepid description he wasn't being truthful with either Señora Garza or himself. Still, he wasn't sure exactly what Marnie was to him or how to describe the relationship between them—a relationship that seemed to become more complex and complicated by the minute. And yet he couldn't bring himself to regret that or to call a halt to it. Some things just had to run their course—and be enjoyed while they did.

"Just a friend?" The other woman grinned gamely, as if sensing his indecision. "She might as well be your sister if that is the case. And what a pity that would be."

"They seem to know you well here," Marnie said once the woman had gone.

"Yeah, well, I try to come in whenever I'm down for an extended stay. The food isn't fancy, but it's tasty and filling. And there's never a wait for a table."

Marnie sipped from one of the bottles of water Señora Garza had left on their table.

"Sounds like you dine in some exclusive places back in California."

He leaned forward, lowered his voice. "Want to know a secret?"

Her brows lifted in surprise. "Will I be killed afterward?"

"Huh?"

"I kind of took you for one of those, 'I'd tell you, but I'd have to kill you' types."

He scowled. "You want to hear this or not?"

"Do tell, please," she said, scooting forward in her chair, settling her elbows on the table and then plopping her chin into her hands. "And spare no details."

"All right. I like fast food."

Marnie slumped back in her seat. "That's not a secret. Or, if it is, then half the population of the United States is in on it. Try again. Tell me something juicy, something, I don't know, *shocking*."

"I'll tell you mine if you tell me yours," he bartered.

"I have no secrets."

"Is that a no?"

She blinked slowly. "More like a spill yours and then we'll see about mine."

"Okay." He thought a moment. "If you hadn't come back, I might have gone looking for you."

He hadn't intended to say that. In fact, he hadn't realized it was true until just that moment, but there was no denying something about Marnie made him want the kinds of things he'd wanted before his divorce when he'd envisioned having a partner and a family, rather than a fashionable accessory to show off at cocktail parties. He'd wanted a lover certainly, but more than that, he'd wanted someone to share his life. All Terri had shared was his bank account and a house so big and showy that it had never felt like a real home.

Since the ugly court battle two years earlier, he'd convinced himself those things just weren't possible any longer. Wealth hadn't changed him, at least he didn't feel it had, but it had changed how others viewed him and treated him.

Then he'd met Marnie—forthright and passionate, silly and sweet. Even riddled with doubts about their relationship, she had him reconsidering the solo life he'd so thoroughly mapped out for himself over the past two-dozen months.

"You would have looked for me? Really?"

He nodded. "And I would have found you."

"That's what you do for a living."

She sounded sad when she said it. The truth perched on his tongue, wanting to take flight.

"What if it wasn't?"

"You're a risk-taker by nature or you wouldn't have gravitated to that profession."

"It bothers you that much?"

Her smile was overly bright. "No. Why would it? We're just…what are we exactly?"

"Haven't figured that out myself."

"More than friends but not quite lovers."

"Yet," he added, after which the talkative, even argumentative Marnie was amazingly silent.

They lodged for the night in a small ten-room motel that overlooked a ravine halfway between Catavina and El Rosario. Phil's Lodge. The name had her baffled until they walked inside. The owner was American or had been before he'd chucked his three-piece suits and migrated south. Now he looked more like a middle-aged surfer than the accountant he'd been.

Marnie hadn't had to request separate rooms. J.T. rented two before she'd even had to ask.

"I can pay for my own," she said, when he handed Phil some bills to cover their tab.

He sent her a wink. "This one's on me."

"Thank you," she said.

Under his breath so that Phil couldn't hear, he said, "You might want to hold your gratitude until after you've seen them."

She thought he had a point when he swung open the door of the two rooms and gave her first dibs.

"The choice is so hard," she said sarcastically.

The rooms, which were right next door to one another, were small and identical. The only furnishings were battered six-drawer bureaus, lamps and lumpy full-size beds, both of which were pushed up against the interior wall the two rooms shared.

"I guess I'll take this one," she said.

J.T. held Marnie's door open for her and she stepped inside, wrinkling her nose at the musty smell.

"It's not much," he apologized, glancing around.

She dropped her backpack onto the bed and shrugged. "It's fine. And, if the water is hot and clear, it's a step up from my accommodations in La Playa de la Pisada."

"And here I thought you were high maintenance," he teased.

She batted her eyelashes. "I get that a lot, and I've never figured out why."

She tried to open the room's only window, but it wouldn't budge.

"Allow me."

After one brawny push, it slid open with a squawk of protest.

"Thanks."

They stood awkwardly in the center of the room for a moment, and then he kissed her, quickly, and left. Next door, she heard his window creak open.

"How's your room?" she asked, not even bothering to raise her voice. "Same pleasing…fragrance?"

He laughed. "Yeah. Eau de mildew."

She heard the creak of bedsprings then and her libido hurdled well ahead of her imagination.

"Wh-what are you doing?" she asked.

He hesitated a moment before replying in a silky voice, "What do you think I'm doing?"

"Laying down?"

"Close. Sitting down and pulling off my hiking boots. I'm going to take a shower. What about you? What are you doing?"

She sank onto the edge of the mattress, smiling when the bedsprings sent up a similarly squeaky chorus. She reached down to untie her dusty sneakers.

"Untying my shoelaces."

"I'm taking off my shirt now," he said as Marnie toed off her shoes.

Smiling, she replied, "Mine unbuttons."

One at a time, she fished the buttons through their holes, keeping him apprised of her slow progress.

"That was the last one. Shirt's off."

"Bra?"

"White lace with a front hook." She hummed as she worked the clasp free and slipped her arms out of the straps. "And there it goes."

As she tossed it onto the heap of clothes, she thought she heard his groan float through the open window. Then the bedsprings creaked again.

"Jeans," he said in a tight voice.

"Shorts." And then she barely waited a beat before upping the ante. With a wiggle that jangled the rusty springs, she added, "And a little silky something that matched the bra."

"Marnie?"

"Yeah?"

"Meet you back here after a shower?"

She swallowed thickly. "Deal."

Fifteen minutes later, they were both lying on their separate beds, talking through their open windows.

"What is the craziest thing you've ever done?" she asked.

"Easy. Laid in a cheap motel room in Mexico with a beautiful woman in the next room and talked through the open window rather than climbing in bed with her and putting us both out of our misery."

She laughed, even as heat shimmied through her belly. "Besides that. Come on, fess up."

"All right. Let's see, craziest thing. Ah, I've

got it. I once mooned a competitor at a trade show when I was young and stupid."

He couldn't believe he'd exposed himself that way—either then or now. Hell, he'd never confided even in his ex-wife about that juvenile prank, and thank God or an embellished account of it no doubt would have wound up in her tell-all book.

But all Marnie said was, "They have trade shows for bounty hunters?"

He hesitated a moment. Maybe he should tell her the truth now. He wanted to and he thought he could trust her with it. But before he could get the words out, she was saying, "Well, don't you want to know my craziest thing?"

"Of course."

He heard the grin in her voice when she said, "I put plastic wrap over the toilets in the teachers' lounge at the middle school. Mary Jane Battle dared me to do it. Caused quite a splash when my social studies teacher went in to relieve himself, if you know what I mean."

Then she laughed, sounding young and carefree and making him feel that way, too. How long had it been since he'd felt either of those things?

"Who knew that the heart of a reprobate beat in that impressive chest of yours?"

"It was just a prank. Not malicious really. Not like the time Mary Jane's brother Brice added a laxative in the brownies his grand-mother made for the county fair."

"*Eew.*"

"Exactly."

"Did the grandma win any blue ribbons?"

"None, but to hear Brice tell it he was black and blue afterward."

They were silent for a few minutes. Then he asked, "What did you put on after your shower?"

"Why do men always want to know what a woman is wearing?"

He chuckled softly into the darkness. "Because we like to torture ourselves."

"Masochist."

"Guilty as charged. Well?"

"Black silk."

Marnie purred out the words, surprised at how easily she could flirt. Surprised by how young and carefree he could make her feel with one simple, silly question.

"How's it look on you?"

"How do you think?"

There was that groan again. "Great. Form-fitting?"

"Like a second skin," she confirmed, grinning as she ran one hand down the loose white cotton tank top she wore. "And remember that lacy little thong that was snagged on the switch of my flashlight the day we first met?"

"You're enjoying this, aren't you?"

"You asked," she reminded him, not bothering to camouflage the smugness she was feeling.

"Want to know what I'm wearing?"

"Sure."

Deep laughter rumbled then and she called herself a dozen kinds of fool when he replied, "Not a thing, unless you count the sheet."

Bedsprings rattled again.

"It's too hot for a sheet," he informed her wickedly, right after which he said, "Pleasant dreams."

In the morning, he knocked at her door dressed in his hiking clothes and bearing coffee, which made it easy to forgive him even though he'd woken her from a sound sleep.

"That doesn't look black," he said, motioning toward the tank top.

She grabbed for the coffee, ignored him until she'd inhaled deeply from the spiral of steam curling over the cup's lip, and then, feeling sufficiently awake said, "And you don't look naked."

"I can get that way," he offered.

She didn't miss a beat. "Coffee's more important to me than a naked man at this point."

"Let me know when that changes."

She brought the cup to her lips, paused. "You'll be the first."

And it scared her only a little to realize that she actually meant it.

He rubbed the back of his neck, but changed the subject when he finally spoke.

"I was wondering if instead of heading back you'd like to head a little further south today, maybe spend another night away from La Playa de la Pisada? Down off Guerrero Negro there's a charter boat company that takes sightseers out whale watching. It's late in the season, but we might get lucky. Ever been?"

"Whale watching?"

He nodded.

"No."

"It's an awesome sight."

"I'd like that," she said, wishing Noah were going with them. Then she handed him the empty coffee cup. "And I'd love another cup of coffee if you'd be so kind."

"Maybe I could round up a Danish, too," he replied.

She chose not to notice the roll of his eyes or the slight sarcasm that had shaded his tone.

"Do they have those down here?" And without waiting for him to answer, she fired off her instructions. "No jelly-filled or plain. But anything coated in chocolate or oozing custard would be okay."

"Thought you were worried about calories?"

"I'll work those off later," she said, enjoying immensely the basic male speculation that flooded his expression. And talk about hunger, the man looked famished.

"I can be ready in fifteen minutes," she said when he just continued to regard her.

That snapped him out of it. "No woman can be ready in a mere fifteen minutes."

She shrugged, knowing in her case at least his chauvinistic response was unfortunately true.

"Yes, but I'll be ready for you to *wait* for me by then."

She turned toward the small bathroom, stopped. Over her shoulder she said, "And I'll be ready for my second cup of coffee, too."

"You're something else," he muttered, but his lips were twitching.

It took Marnie forty minutes to get ready, but only because she knew J.T. was sitting on her bed, foot tapping and glancing at his watch.

And maybe it took her that long because she wanted to look her best, she admitted, assessing her appearance in the small mirror.

She'd pulled on a sleeveless blouse over a crimson bra. The lacy-edged underwire gave her figure support as well spilling a generous amount of cleavage into the V of the shirt, the buttons of which she'd left undone one lower than she normally dared. The blouse tied at the waist over a pair of tan hiking shorts that were snug across her rear and short enough to show off her slim thighs, which were nicely tanned now. After applying a minimal amount of makeup, she pulled her hair back into a ponytail, slid a pair of small hoop earrings through the holes in her lobes and smiled at her reflection.

He stood when she walked out of the bath-room.

"Ready," she announced.

His gaze slid down, stopping just below her shoulders, as she knew it would.

"And worth the wait," he replied, tugging her to him for a kiss.

The springs squawked like a flock of wounded geese when they tumbled together onto the bed.

"No need to go out on some boat when we

could view the wonder of nature up close and personal from right here," he suggested.

Her breathing was no more even than his when she scooted out from beneath his solid body and stood.

"Whales."

He scrubbed a hand over his face.

"Right."

CHAPTER TEN

MARNIE sat on the beach in La Playa de la Pisada a week later, watching the waves heave against the shore. She felt that way, too: Restless and on edge.

And yet not ready to move on.

Only a couple of days remained of her time in Mexico. It had gone by so quickly with all she and J.T. had packed into the past week. In fact, just the day before they'd traveled to Ensenada again, where they'd visited la Punta Banda Peninsula on the Bay of Todos Los Santas. They'd stood near La Bufadora and let the spray from the marine geyser rain down on them.

Still laughing and soaked to the skin, they'd

eaten at an outdoor café in town, warmed by the sun and each other's company. Marnie had paid for their meal. She'd insisted. He'd been far too generous with her already, always surprising her with a trinket or souvenir from the places they stopped. It had been dark when they'd returned to La Playa de la Pisada. They'd said good-night at her door, both exhausted from another day of sightseeing and heightened sexual tension.

But as quickly as the week had flown, Marnie felt as if she had been gone forever. She'd spoken to her mother just that morning during a trip into town to pick up something special for dessert. She wanted to surprise J.T. that evening, celebrate…something.

"You've been gone a long time."

It hadn't been a criticism, but she'd heard worry in her mother's voice. As a parent herself, she recognized it easily enough and so she apologized for being the cause.

"I've met someone," she added afterward.

She hadn't intended to say anything to her parents about J.T. She might be in her thirties, but parents were parents whatever their offspring's age. And talk about handing them a reason for concern.

Sure enough, her mother's tone was now tinged with alarm.

"Someone from there?" she asked, sounding as if Marnie had called to say she wouldn't be returning at all and to ask that her belongings be shipped south of the border post haste.

"No, although he does own a place here on the peninsula. He's American, Mom. He's… nice."

"Marnie—"

But she'd cut off her mother's words, knowing she wouldn't like what the older woman had to say on the subject and wishing she'd kept this information to herself.

"I'm not going to run away with him or anything, Mother. Promise. It's just a harmless holiday flirtation. That's all it is."

And, for a moment, she almost wished that were the case. How much easier it would be to accept his lifestyle then. How much easier it would be to walk away at the end of her time in Mexico.

Her mother was silent for a long moment, presumably gathering her thoughts. Marnie gave the older woman high marks for changing the subject when she spoke again. Were the roles reversed, she knew she wouldn't have let it drop quite so easily.

"Noah's missed you."

Marnie felt her heart squeeze at the mention of her son. She'd never been away from him for more than a night before this.

"No more than I've missed him," she said as her vision blurred. "Give him and Dad a hug for me. I'll see you all on Sunday."

"Marnie?"

"Yes."

"Take care."

"Always."

"Don't do something you'll…regret."

Sifting a handful of sand between her fingers, Marnie replayed the conversation in her head now as she sat on the beach. Too late, she thought. She already had plenty of regrets when it came to J.T. And, interestingly enough, almost of all them pertained to what the pair of them had managed *not* to do together.

A seabird screamed overhead, swooping low before soaring back up into the darkening sky. As Marnie watched it, she mused that the one thing she didn't regret was revealing her long-dormant dream to J.T.

On the long drive back from whale watching in Guerrero Negro nearly a week ago, they'd discussed her plans for Marnie's Closet at length. He was an excellent sounding board, she'd discovered, full of marketing strategies and advice on ways to get the most out of her initial investment. Indeed, he seemed to possess incredible business acumen. And it had zapped her again, that sizzle of attraction for the intelligent, interesting man God had so thoughtfully tucked inside that hunky exterior. Talk about the complete package.

Gazing out at the horizon, she noted storm clouds were rolling in. Fat and dark, they would soon blot out what little sunshine remained. In the distance, she thought she saw a stab of lightning and sighed, resigned. The electricity had finally come back on in her rental the day before and she knew without a doubt the storm would take it out again once it broke shore. She'd spent so much of her time with J.T. and at his home it really didn't matter, she supposed.

The slamming of a car door startled her and she glanced across the beach in time to see a suit-clad man alight from a dark-colored sedan.

Who is that?

J.T. hadn't received a single visitor the entire time she'd been in La Playa de la Pisada, and even if he had, this absurdly buttoned-up newcomer would have struck her as a fish out of water. Clearly he wasn't here on vacation and his neatly trimmed auburn hair and pale skin told her he wasn't a local. Indeed, everything about him seemed to scream uptight American businessman, the sort that didn't take vacations because they didn't have a life outside their jobs.

As she watched him, he marched to the door of J.T.'s bungalow in his shiny black wingtips and, without bothering to knock, yanked it open and stepped inside.

That capped it for Marnie. Curiosity fully aroused, she stood, shook the sand out of her towel and secured it around her hips over her bathing suit. She'd just go over and have a little look-see. She needed to firm up their plans for dinner anyway, she told herself when her conscience protested that she should mind her own business and give J.T. time alone with his unexpected guest.

She'd barely taken a dozen steps when she heard shouting and decided this was no time for a self-proclaimed busybody to show restraint.

"Dammit, J.T.! You can't hide away here forever. The Justice Department is building a case and that fact isn't going to disappear just because *you* have for the past several weeks. Legal is up to its eyeballs in this mess and has been since before you decided to extend your stay in Mexico," the mystery man thundered.

Whoever he was, he certainly had nerve. And what was this business about the Justice Department? Did J.T. do work for them?

"I don't need your permission to take a vacation, Rick."

J.T.'s voice was quiet in comparison to his guest's and all the more lethal because of its low pitch. She'd never heard him sound so angry, even when they'd first met and he'd peppered her with questions about who she was and her motives for coming to town.

"I didn't say you did, but it's not like you to ignore repeated e-mails and faxes," the other man said.

Marnie peaked through the window as he spoke and noticed from his profile that his face was nearly the color of merlot. Did men in their thirties have strokes? she wondered absently. He seemed well on his way to major health problems with his Type A personality.

He was about J.T.'s age, although not quite as tall, and he might have been good looking if his face weren't quite so pinched, his auburn hair quite so perfectly clipped and gelled into place.

Takes life too seriously, was her first impression. Then: He needs to have a woman run her fingers through that hair until it's good and unruly.

He wasn't another bounty hunter. That much seemed clear. And the conversation she'd overheard had her baffled, what with talk of the Justice Department and a case being built.

"I've been busy," J.T. snarled.

"You can't afford to be too busy right now, my friend."

The man J.T. had called Rick turned then and caught sight of Marnie through the window.

"I believe you have company," he told J.T. as he opened the door to let her in.

Marnie swore J.T. paled when he saw her. But he smiled and held out a hand, bringing her to his side.

"Hello. We didn't see you there."

Her gaze drifted from one man to the other as the tension snapped in the small kitchen like a live electrical wire.

"Just came over to see about our plans for this evening, but I can come back later. I seem to be interrupting something."

"Nothing that can't wait," J.T. said succinctly, to which the other man scowled.

An awkward silence ensued, and Marnie realized J.T. didn't intend to introduce the pair of them. So she offered a hand. "I'm Marnie LaRue, by the way. I've rented the place just up the beach from here."

"Richard Danton. I work—"

"Rick was just leaving," J.T. interrupted.

Rick held J.T.'s icy glare for a moment before snagging his briefcase off the counter. She assumed the man had driven down from California—the plates on his car told her as much—and yet he hadn't even bothered to loosen his tie or unfasten the top button of the snowy shirt he wore. If the air-conditioning in his automobile gave out, she had little doubt he would suffer heat stroke before shrugging out of his charcoal gray suit coat.

"At least look over the papers and get back to me by the end of the week." After a glance at Marnie, Rick added meaningfully, "And make this your top priority, please."

"Don't presume to tell me how to do my

job." J.T.'s voice was as sharp as a surgeon's scalpel.

Rick shook his head, seeming piqued and defeated at the same time.

"Wouldn't dream of it."

On the wall next to him was a small photograph Marnie knew J.T.'s sister, Anne, had taken. The frame was slightly askew. Rick pushed it back into alignment with the tip of his index finger, the gesture seeming almost one of reverence.

Without looking at J.T., he added quietly, "I know my place."

He walked out the door then, which J.T. slammed behind him. Marnie waited until the car was gone from view before she said a word.

"Everything okay?"

J.T. stalked to the window in the main living area, feet planted shoulder-width apart as he stood with his back to her and gazed out at the churning ocean.

"Define okay," he snorted.

His mood didn't appear to have improved any with Rick Danton's departure.

"Oh, 'within tolerance,' as my dad would say."

"Ah, then I suppose so." He turned slowly, his expression grim. "I can't stay here much longer, Marnie. I've got to get back to work."

Questions, dozens of them, beckoned, but she decided to ignore them for the time being.

"I know. Me, too." She tried to smile. "We both knew Mexico wasn't forever."

"Did we?" he asked quietly.

She felt the air back up in her lungs. "Didn't we?"

"Rick's a…lawyer I work with. He was just here reminding me of some important developments back home."

"Duty calls?"

"Something like that." He ran a hand over the back of his neck. "I feel I owe you an ex-

planation about what I do for a living. I haven't
been completely truthful with you."

Curious as she was, Marnie suddenly didn't
want to know, because something in his sol-
emn expression told her it was something
more than just chasing bail jumpers, maybe
something even more dangerous.

"I haven't asked for an explanation."

"No, you haven't." He walked toward her,
stopping just shy of touching her. "You've
taken me at face value. I don't know that
you'll ever understand what that's meant to
me."

Blissful as she decided ignorance could be,
she had to know this much, "Are you in trouble with the law?"

He shook his head. "Not how you mean. It's
a long story."

"But you do have something to hide."

"Nothing bad. Nothing I'm ashamed of, I
can promise you that."

He reached for her hands, held them loosely

in his, but his gaze was direct, his tone urgent when he said, "You once asked me who I was and I told you, 'Just a man.' That's who I am, Marnie. At the very heart of it and no matter what you discover about me later on, please remember I'm just a man."

His words should have frightened her, should have made her pull away. But Marnie didn't want to pull away. In fact, she discovered what she really wanted to do was hold on. And she knew why. It hit her with all of the force of the storm gathering outside. She loved him.

"You'll never be *just* a man to me," she whispered, rising on tiptoe to kiss his cheek.

"Aw, Marnie."

He held her tightly against him as if she were a lifeline that had been tossed in to save him. Some of the tension seemed to ebb from his frame, but it flooded back when he spoke again.

"I'm leaving in the morning."

He didn't speak of the days that would come after that, or of what place she would have in his life in the future. Once—was it just days ago?—J.T. had told her he would have come after her when she tried to leave Mexico the first time. He didn't say any such thing now.

And even though she loved him, she wasn't sure she wanted him to.

Here, they could be Marnie and J.T. But back in the States—back in the *real world* where work obligations and family responsibilities beckoned—they would be two entirely different people, living on opposite sides of the country, pursuing different goals. It seemed doubtful their lives could fit together so seamlessly then.

Even if the matter of logistics could be solved, Marnie was a small-town single mother determined to build a business and establish financial security for her son. How could she make a life with a man who traveled the globe not to mention who came with so many secrets? And, of course, she had kept a secret of her own: Noah.

She had no idea how J.T. would feel about her son or about her being a mother. A lot of men didn't want the baggage that came with an instant family. Perhaps, she admitted, that hadn't been her only reason for not mentioning Noah. Like J.T., she had enjoyed being just a woman. But she knew better than anyone that such a simplified fantasy could not last.

And she had a feeling she wasn't the only one having second thoughts. Already, something about J.T. had changed. He seemed resigned, weary, even a little remote. Was he already pulling back, stepping away from her?

Marnie felt her heart break even as she reached her decision. Her life was in Chance Harbor with her son. Noah would always come first. But for tonight, for just this one night, as much as she abhorred risk, she would gamble more than the heart she had already lost to J.T.

"I'll be leaving tomorrow, too." She reached for his hand and started back through the small house. At his bedroom door he tugged her to a stop.

"Marnie?"

She laid a finger to his lips. "Let's make the most of tonight."

They made love as the storm built outside, its vengeful fists pounding on the roof and rattling the windows, and the intensity of their emotions matched the raging weather. Hours later, once the storm had passed and the thunder echoed low in the distance, they made love again. It was this slow and sweet good-bye Marnie knew she would remember forever.

She woke before daylight wrapped in J.T.'s strong arms, with her body fitted snugly, intimately against his big warm one. She wanted to stay there, wanted it so badly that she made herself scoot out of his embrace. Then she dressed and slipped from the room.

Was she making the right decision? It hurt so much to leave, she decided it must be.

After Hal's death, she had been consumed with anxiety, most of it irrational. She'd worried about everyone she loved, fretting over Mason and Rose's safety when they were in the state capital while the Legislature was in session; checking on Noah countless times during the night until she'd become a walking zombie.

She could look back now and admit such worrying was excessive and in direct relation to the loss she'd suffered. But she felt it bubbling back to the surface now. And with J.T., the reasons seemed valid enough. She couldn't live like this. Call her a fool, call her spineless, she couldn't wake up each day wondering if he would come home to her that night.

In his kitchen, she found a piece of scrap paper and pen.

What words were there to write? she wondered dimly. She started with the ones she'd wanted to say last night, the three words that had pitched and hurled about inside her head while he'd undressed her and then followed her down onto the soft mattress of his bed.

I love you.

She followed that declaration with the infamous conjunction:

But I don't expect anything more from you than what we shared last night. We're different people, with different goals and different needs, but I'll never regret my time with you in Mexico.

Things here were simple. You were, as you said, just a man. And I got to be just a woman. But that's not all that I am. You asked me who I was when we met and I never really told you. Not all of it. I'm not just a widow. I'm also a mother. I have a son, J.T., a four-year-old boy who depends on me for everything. I've been away too long already, but it felt so good to be here, so good to clear my head and dream again.

I'm going to start my business. Thank you for all of your advice and encouragement. I'd forgotten how to want things for myself over the past few years, how to take risks. But ultimately what I want and what I'm willing to risk are subordinate to what my son needs from me: Stability.

He needs to know I will be there for him physically and emotionally. I cannot do that if I am consumed by worry for you.

I wish you the best always. Please stay safe.

Love, Marnie

She left the note on the kitchen table propped up on the seashells she'd collected during their many walks, and she slipped out the door as the sun scaled the horizon in the east to bathe the beach in its pale golden light.

J.T. read the note for a third time, his reaction remaining identical to the two previous times he'd done so. He wanted to punch something.

Marnie was gone.

More than her note confirmed that fact. Her car no longer was parked outside the little shack down the beach, which looked all the more desolate and disreputable now.

She'd left him. He still couldn't quite believe it. After last night and all they had shared together, she'd walked out on him that morning without letting him explain, without bothering to wake him and say goodbye. He glanced at the empty coffeepot on the counter. Hell, she'd been in such a hurry to go she hadn't even had her morning jolt of caffeine first. If that didn't say it all!

He went outside and slumped into one of the chairs on the patio. Women had walked out on him before. His wife, in fact, on their fifth wedding anniversary, right after informing him that she and the team of shrewd lawyers she'd hired with his money planned to take him to cleaners.

He'd felt angry then, hurt and betrayed. But those emotions were nothing compared to what was churning inside of him right now.

And yet, what had he expected? That Marnie would stay in La Playa de la Pisada until *he* could leave *her?* Was his ego such that it demanded he be the one to walk away?

He sighed. No, either way, parting would have been painful. And necessary.

But was it? For the first time since his divorce, he questioned his decision to remain single. Terri's infidelity and duplicity had left him suspicious and unable to trust the women he'd met after her, especially since he believed his bank account had often been the main draw. But sassy, self-sufficient Marnie didn't know anything about his billions. She didn't know about his California estate or the other homes he owned in Aspen and Paris. She didn't know anything about Tracker Operating Systems.

She didn't know about those things because J.T. hadn't told her. He'd had excuses for remaining mum. They'd seemed valid enough at the time despite being self-serving, but ultimately it all boiled down to one thing: He hadn't trusted her. Well, he decided, stuffing the note into the pocket of his shorts, maybe it was time he trusted his heart.

CHAPTER ELEVEN

MARNIE wiped down the mahogany bar that swept along the back wall of the Lighthouse Tavern and then refilled the dishes of beer nuts. It was a light evening, even for a Monday. Only a couple of the regulars had bothered to brave the freezing rain outside to come in for refreshments and a friendly game of pool.

Brice Battle was racking the balls as his brother Brad selected a cue stick, but even this infamously loud duo seemed subdued.

"Another round?" Marnie called to them.

"Sure." Brice pointed to his brother and grinned gamely. "On him. He's going to lose. Again."

Good-natured ribbing ensued, but Marnie tuned it out. Her thoughts strayed to J.T. and Mexico and that golden stretch of beach that she'd come to consider a small slice of heaven. It had been just over two weeks since she'd returned from her vacation. Since then, she'd resisted the urge to slip back into her old life. Instead she'd begun making changes, up-ending the status quo with plans for her business.

She delivered drinks to the Battle brothers and lowered herself into a chair at a nearby table where Bergen, the tavern's surly cook, sat finishing up a burger.

"I should be at home, in front of my potbellied stove, warming my toes. This is my last Michigan winter," he groused, even though technically it was already spring.

"You say that every year."

"This time I mean it."

She patted his leathery cheek—knowing full well she was one of the few people who could get away with such a gesture. "And you say that every year, too."

"You're just full of sass since coming back from Mexico," he commented, swatting her hand when she reached out to steal a fry off his plate.

"And you missed my smart mouth."

Distracting him with a dazzling smile, she not only filched a fry, she dunked it in the small mound of catsup on his plate.

The scowl mellowed on Bergen's craggy face. "I did. I've worried plenty over you since Hal's been gone."

"I worried about me, too. But I'm better now or at least heading in that direction."

"Glad to hear it." And he actually smiled.

"Thanks, Bergen." Unable to help herself, she sniffled.

"Oh jeez!" He tossed down the last bite of his burger and rose to his feet. To no one in particular, he said, "Say one nice thing and she gets all emotional. Forget I mentioned it."

But before he stalked off in the direction of the kitchen, he handed her his hankie.

Marnie dabbed at her eyes and watched Brice sink a ball into one of the pool table's corner pockets. Bergen was right. She had some of her sass back. She felt hopeful, ready to take chances again. In fact, hadn't she already taken a huge gamble when she'd given herself—heart and body—to J.T. that last night in Mexico?

It dawned on her then, slapping her with as much force as the cue ball that Brice used to send another striped one down a side pocket. Leaving J.T. hadn't lessened her anxiety. If anything, it had intensified it.

Where was he now? What was he doing? And, above all, was he safe? She'd lain awake every night of the past two weeks wondering, worrying.

Math had never been her strong suit, but Marnie could add up this easily enough. She could have J.T. in her life and worry about him, or she could stay away from him and worry about him just as much. Only one side of that equation offered something positive in return for both her and Noah.

She sucked in a breath as the truth dawned as bright and welcoming as the sun had been on that beach in Mexico. She wanted J.T. in her life no matter what. They'd figure a way around the obstacles. They'd have to.

"Oh my God!" she hollered.

At which Brice scratched and swore lavishly.

"Sorry," she called, but she was laughing, the wheels of her mind already turning.

She had to find J.T. before she could convince him he couldn't live without her. The convincing part would be easy and mutually satisfying, she decided with a grin. Finding him, however, might not be so simple. He no longer would be in Mexico and all she knew was that he lived in California. Of course, she did know his photographer sister lived in San

Francisco. She could start there, contacting galleries until she found one that carried Anne Lundy's work.

Mason, as a former private investigator, might have some other ideas. The door to the tavern jangled open as she mulled her options, and her brother strode through as if on cue. His wife, Rose, was right behind him, looking as happy and lovely as ever, despite the spitting cold outside.

Marnie smiled broadly. "This is a surprise. I thought you were heading back to Lansing. The taxpayers might not take too kindly to your taking four-day weekends."

"Tell it to the weather. They're talking about closing the Mac tonight," Mason said, referring to the five-mile-long suspension bridge that linked Michigan's two peninsulas.

She squinted a look out the cloudy windows. "It's that bad out?"

"High winds, ice." Mason shrugged. "What would May on Superior's shore be without one last blast of winter? We'll head out in the morning, assuming the weather has cleared. We've come to ask you a favor."

"Really? How interesting?" And convenient, she decided, since she was about to do the same.

"I've got an important committee meeting in the afternoon that I really don't want to miss. Rose and I are planning to fly down to Lansing, leave our car here. We were wondering if you could drive us to the airport in Houghton in the morning, maybe pick us back up next weekend?"

"Of course. And I have a favor to ask of you."

"That smile on your face is making me nervous," he replied. "What is it?"

But she never got out the words. She glanced up at the television perched in the corner and nearly fainted.

J.T.'s handsome face filled the screen. His cheeks were free of the golden stubble he'd often sported in Mexico and his hair had been trimmed and was neatly combed back from his face. He wore a suit and looked as if he could be a banker or some sort of executive. But it was J.T. No doubt about it.

"Oh my God!" Marnie cried for the second time that evening. This time, it was fear that had her heart bucking against her ribs. What had happened to make him the lead story on the evening news?

"Wh—" Mason began only to be shushed into silence.

"Give me the remote, the *remote!*" Marnie hollered, flapping her hand toward where it sat on the end of the bar.

Mason grabbed the remote and tossed it to her. She turned up the volume as she slid bonelessly into a chair.

"The Justice Department announced today that after reviewing hundreds of documents and internal memos, it is dropping its antitrust lawsuit against Tracker Operating Systems.

Company founder and president Jonathan Thomas Lundy had this to say:

"I'm relieved, of course, but I knew that Tracker had done nothing wrong and ultimately would be vindicated."

The rest of his statement was lost to the loud buzzing in Marnie's ears. *Jonathan Thomas* Lundy? *Founder and president* of Tracker Operating Systems?

Hysterical laughter bubbled to the surface. To think she'd once told him he should consider a career in computers if the bounty-hunting thing didn't work out.

Laughter ebbed and she dipped her head to rap it lightly against the top of the table.

"I'm such a fool."

"Do you know him?" Rose asked, coming to sit next to her.

"No. She doesn't know Lundy," Mason scoffed, dropping into the seat on the other side of her. Then, "Do you?"

"We met in Mexico. I didn't realize who he was."

"That's nothing to be upset about. A lot of people wouldn't recognize him," Rose said.

"Sure," Mason piped in. "So you didn't know who he was. What's the big deal?"

"You don't understand. I didn't just *meet* him. I...I *slept* with him," Marnie cried softly.

Mason sucked in a breath and stood.

"Too much information. *Way* too much information," he said, tucking his hands into the front pockets of his jeans and walking several paces away.

"Oh, put your big brother sensibilities on hold for a moment," Rose admonished. Turning to Marnie, she asked, "Do you love him?"

"Yes. Before you guys walked in I was sitting here plotting a way to find him. You were going to help me, by the way," she said, sparing a glance at her brother, whose cheeks were still tinted pink.

"And I can see why you'd need me," Mason

remarked dryly. "I mean, it would be so hard to track down a man whose name is synonymous with computers."

"Hush!" Rose said. Then, to Marnie, "Does he love you?"

"I thought so, even though he never said the actual words. But apparently not. He didn't tell me who he was. *Friends call me J.T.,*" she mimicked. "He never mentioned that those friends head up the Fortune 500."

"Maybe those weren't the friends he was talking about," Rose said.

His words came back to Marnie then: *I'm just a man. No matter what you hear about me later, remember that I'm just a man.*

Uh-huh, just a man. *Just a man worth billions!* He obviously hadn't trusted her with the truth.

"I feel like such an idiot," she said.

By two in the morning, Marnie was past feeling like an idiot and had moved on to heat-seeking-missile mad. Noah was sleeping peacefully as she sat at her computer, with its Tracker Operating System no less, surfing the world wide web. She plugged in J.T.'s full name and with the stroke of a key Google spat back scads of hits. She clicked on the one that had her temper flaring all over again.

Last month, while the pair of them had cavorted on a beach in Mexico, the readers of one of America's leading celebrity magazines had dubbed J.T. the World's Sexiest CEO. In fact, the poll noted, that hunky Jonathan Thomas Lundy had topped the list for the second straight year!

The snake.

The cad.

And was that a Saville Row suit he was wearing in the accompanying photo?

Just a man, indeed!

She was still royally ticked off the next morning as she and Noah stood in Houghton's small airport and waited for Mason and Rose's flight to board.

It was not quite nine o'clock and she'd gotten only a few hours of fitful sleep the night before, which is why she had sent Mason in the direction of the airport's small café and instructed him not to return until he could bring her a cup of freshly brewed coffee, the stronger the better. And God help him if he brought back anything diluted with cream or a flavored nondairy product.

"Here you are. The perfect cup of coffee."

She turned, expecting to find her brother, but it was J.T. Lundy who stood in front of her holding out the white-capped foam cup as if it were a peace offering.

He looked the same as he had the night before when she'd seen him on the television, except the suit he wore was now a little wrinkled, the perfectly knotted tie pulled loose and his cheeks were shaded with stubble.

She sucked in a breath, tamping down on the urge to grin and hop into his arms.

Resting her hands on her hips, she demanded instead, "What kind of beans?"

"French roast."

"Did you add any creamer?"

"No, ma'am. It's black. The way God intended a good cup of coffee to be—or so someone once told me."

"Hmm. Thank you."

She took the cup and walked over to a nearby bank of chairs, where she sat, regal as a queen holding court.

This wasn't going well, J.T. decided, smiling uncomfortably at the man, woman and small boy who now regarded him with open curiosity.

The man held out a hand. "Mason Striker. I'm Marnie's brother. And this is my wife, Rose."

"J.T. Nice to meet you both."

"And I'm Noah." The little boy tugged on

his arm. "I'm four. And I think you're in big trouble."

J.T. saw Marnie in the small boy's slow-blinking eyes. And, God help him, he tumbled for the son just as he had for the mother.

Squatting down in front of him, J.T. asked, "Why do you think I'm in trouble?"

"Mom's doing the thing with her lips. She only does that when I've done something really bad."

J.T. glanced over and, sure enough, Marnie's lips were pursed together tighter than the seal on Fort Knox.

"I see what you mean. What do you suggest I do?"

"Better 'pologize."

"Do you think that will work?"

The little boy gazed at him thoughtfully for a moment and then said with devastating honesty, "Probably not right away, but it's a good start."

"Well, here goes nothing."

"We'll wait right here," Rose said, snagging Noah by the hand when he fell into step beside J.T.

"Good luck," Mason called. And unless J.T. missed his guess, the man was laughing at him.

He settled into the seat next to Marnie, who ignored him and sipped the hot beverage.

"Coffee okay?"

"Fine."

"Surprised to see me?"

She shrugged, noncommittal, and took another sip.

"Aren't you even going to ask me why I'm here?"

"Not interested, *Jonathan*." But after saying that, she turned and jabbed an index finger into the center of his chest.

"Bounty hunter, my butt!" she hollered loud enough for the dozen or so people milling about the terminal to glance their way. "You couldn't even track down the truth, pal."

She's not going to make this easy, he realized. But then, this *was* Marnie LaRue. She'd never make anything easy. She'd never hold back her opinion. She'd speak her mind, regardless of the consequences.

And wasn't that why he was here? J.T. thought. Wasn't that why he'd spent the past twenty-four hours in various airports waiting out bad weather until he could get to this little speck in the Lower Forty-Eight? And how his heart had squeezed with disbelief and joy when he'd spotted Marnie in the waiting area.

He'd wanted to believe she'd somehow known he was arriving and had come to the airport to greet him. But the tight clench of her jaw told him otherwise.

"I found the truth. It took me a while, but I found it." He reached for the hand that she'd poked him with, holding it firmly when she tried to tug it free.

"I love you, Marnie LaRue."

The words left him exposed, vulnerable.

Marnie blinked slowly, but didn't say a word. In the silence that ensued, J.T. thought he heard Mason mutter, "God help him."

"I love you," he repeated more forcefully this time.

"You love me?"

"I do."

"The man's toast," Mason declared. Marnie glared at her brother before transferring her glacial gaze to J.T.

"And I'm supposed to believe this after you lied to me about something as basic as your occupation?"

"Yes. And I'm sorry about misleading you. I wanted to level with you."

"Then why didn't you?"

"I tried that on the last night."

"What about before then?"

"I guess I liked being anonymous and having you enjoy my company anyway."

"Just a man," she murmured.

"Yes."

"Couldn't you have at least mentioned that you were *just a man who had founded a billion-dollar computer software empire?*"

"Would that fact have made you love me more or less?" he challenged.

"Don't do that."

"What?"

"Act all self-righteous. I've got the corner on self-righteous right now, Mr. Sexiest CEO."

He winced. "Saw that, huh?"

"Yep. The article I read on-line last night said that that particular title has been bestowed on you twice now. If I hadn't been in such a funk the past few years, I'm sure I would have put it all together while we were still in Mexico."

"I'm glad you didn't."

"It comes down to trust, J.T. And you didn't trust me."

He nodded once.

"It wasn't just you I didn't trust. I didn't trust myself. I loved my ex-wife, but she made it clear when she left that the only thing she'd ever been interested in was my money. Since my divorce, I haven't hurt for female companionship, but those women all knew me as Jonathan Lundy. I could never be sure if they liked me or just my money." He snorted out a laugh. "Want to know what I liked about you from the start?"

"Hmm?"

"Your bluntness."

"That's Marnie," Mason agreed.

"This is a private conversation," Marnie called over. "Do you mind?"

"Not at all." To J.T., Mason said, "When I was proposing to Rose, she butted in throughout the conversation."

"Then turnabout is fair play," J.T. replied, shocking everyone into silence when he lowered himself to one knee in front of Marnie.

"As soon as you left Mexico, I knew I'd be coming after you, but that business with the Justice Department needed to be settled first.

I love you, Marnie LaRue. You're smart and funny and sweet."

"Is he talking about my sister?" Mason asked, then sucked in a breath when Rose elbowed him in the ribs.

"And you have one hell of a right hook."

"Yep, that's Marnie." Mason muttered, but he was grinning now and so was Rose.

"Will you marry me?"

"What about a prenuptial agreement?" Marnie asked, raising her chin in challenge.

"No need. I don't just trust myself and what I'm feeling, I trust you. All that I have is yours."

Marnie swallowed hard. If she'd had any doubts about his feelings, they would have evaporated right then and there. He loved her. Her grin was slow in coming, though. Make him wait. That had always been her mantra.

"Actually, when I mentioned the prenup, I was thinking about my business. Marnie's Closet is going to be huge."

J.T. pinched his eyes shut. "Is there a 'yes' in there someplace?"

"Yes!" Rose called out for her.

"I think he wants to hear me say it," Marnie chuckled.

J.T. opened his eyes. "Well? Will you marry me, Marnie LaRue?"

He pulled out a ring with a rock big enough to make the Hope diamond look like a mere chip. Marnie fanned her face and sucked in a deep breath.

"Oh, my."

"Getting warmer," he coaxed. Then he sobered. "Life doesn't hold any guarantees. You probably know that better than anyone. But I can make you one. For every day we have together, I'll love you and try to make you happy. Noah, too." He lowered his voice so that only she could hear. "I'll love him like my own, Marnie. I promise you that, too. He's yours, so how could I not?"

"Oh, J.T."

He caught the tears that spilled over onto her cheeks, brushing them away with his fingertips.

"You're a good man."

J.T. cocked up one sandy eyebrow. "And a patient one. I'm still waiting to hear that three-letter word."

"But my answer contains only two letters."

He sucked in a breath. "Two?"

"*Si.*"

"Excuse me?"

"*Si,*" she repeated, trying to tuck away her grin and failing miserably. "It means yes in Spanish."

"I know what it means."

"Well, then I think you should kiss me. That's usually how these proposal things work. The man asks and once the woman gets around to saying yes, the man ki—"

J.T. didn't let Marnie get the rest of the words out.

But Noah summed things up perfectly for everyone. "And then they all live happily ever after."

MILLS & BOON® PUBLISH EIGHT LARGE PRINT TITLES A MONTH. THESE ARE THE EIGHT TITLES FOR JANUARY 2006

———— ❧ ————

THE RAMIREZ BRIDE
Emma Darcy

EXPOSED: THE SHEIKH'S MISTRESS
Sharon Kendrick

THE SICILIAN MARRIAGE
Sandra Marton

AT THE FRENCH BARON'S BIDDING
Fiona Hood-Stewart

THEIR NEW-FOUND FAMILY
Rebecca Winters

THE BILLIONAIRE'S BRIDE
Jackie Braun

CONTRACTED: CORPORATE WIFE
Jessica Hart

IMPOSSIBLY PREGNANT
Nicola Marsh

MILLS & BOON®

Live the emotion

MILLS & BOON® PUBLISH EIGHT LARGE PRINT TITLES A MONTH. THESE ARE THE EIGHT TITLES FOR FEBRUARY 2006

❦

THE BRAZILIAN'S BLACKMAILED BRIDE
Michelle Reid

EXPECTING THE PLAYBOY'S HEIR
Penny Jordan

THE TYCOON'S TROPHY WIFE
Miranda Lee

WEDDING VOW OF REVENGE
Lucy Monroe

MARRIAGE AT MURRAREE
Margaret Way

WINNING BACK HIS WIFE
Barbara McMahon

JUST FRIENDS TO...JUST MARRIED
Renee Roszel

THE SHOCK ENGAGEMENT
Ally Blake

MILLS & BOON®

Live the emotion

0106 Rom LP